LARGE PRINT
F   1988   126195
            c1959
COBURN, WALT
BRANDED   4/aa
                     Withdrawn

Fic.
Coburn, Walt,
Branded
WILLARD LIB   86019803

3 4420 99015552 5

Willard Memorial Library
Willard, Ohio

RULES

1. Books may be kept two weeks and may be renewed for the same period.

2. A fine of three cents a day will be charged on each book which is not returned according to the above rule. No book will be issued to any person incurring such a fine until it has been paid.

3. All injuries to books beyond reasonable wear and all losses shall be made good to the satisfaction of the Librarian.

4. Each borrower is held responsible for all books drawn on his card and for all fines accruing on the same.

LARGE PRINT Western

BRANDED

Pete could trust no one. Certainly not his outlaw father, who had abandoned him to the crazed rancher Zee Dunbar. Not Zee's pretty wife Tracy either—she was too free with her attentions to too many men. He couldn't trust Montana law—which wanted to see him hang. All that he *could* trust was the lightning-fast draw of his six-shooter. But he was to learn that wasn't enough—that a man could save his skin yet lose his soul to a destiny far worse than death—if he didn't trust someone!

BRANDED

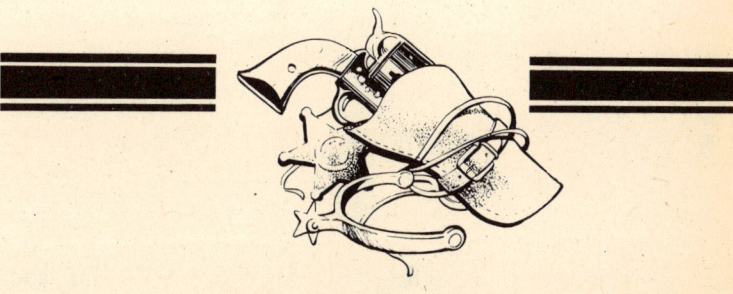

Walt Coburn

WILLARD MEMORIAL LIBRARY
WILLARD, OH 44890
CLASS NO. F
ACCESSION NO. 126195

ATLANTIC LARGE PRINT
Chivers Press, Bath, England.
John Curley & Associates Inc.,
South Yarmouth, Mass., USA.

Library of Congress Cataloging-in-Publication Data

Coburn, Walt, 1889–1971.
  Branded.

  1. large type books.   I. Title
[PS3505.O153B7 1987]   813'.52   86–19803
ISBN 1–55504–215–5 (pbk.:lg. print)

British Library Cataloguing in Publication Data

Coburn, Walt
  Branded.—Large print ed.—(Atlantic
  large print)
  I. Title
  813'.52[F]   PS3505.O153

  ISBN 0–7451–9212–2

This Large Print edition is published by Chivers Press, England, and John Curley & Associates, Inc, U.S.A. 1987

Published by arrangement with Donald MacCampbell, Inc

U.K. Hardback ISBN 0 7451 9212 2
U.S.A. Softback ISBN 1 55504 215 5

Copyright © 1959 by Walt Coburn
All rights reserved

Photoset, printed and bound in Great Britain by
REDWOOD BURN LIMITED, Trowbridge, Wiltshire

BRANDED

CHAPTER ONE

It was typical of Zee Dunbar to wait six or seven years until Booger Red Craven built up his Boxed X outfit in the Montana badlands, with a long rope and a running-iron, into a sizeable cow spread, before he closed in on the tough cattle rustler.

Booger Red and his eighteen-year-old son Pete had twenty-five head of big weaned and unbranded calves in the pole corral. Pete was heating half a dozen branding irons in the fire about daybreak. He had a big, smoke-blackened coffee-pot at the edge of the bed of hot ashes, letting the coffee simmer while he waited for the irons to get a cherry red.

Booger Red had a 30–30 saddle carbine cradled in the crook of his left arm as he led his horse across the corral to the branding fire. He was a six-foot, raw-boned man with a week's growth of greying red beard and a pair of narrowed, bloodshot, green eyes and a splayed nose that had been broken and badly set. There was an old knife scar that ridged from one eyebrow to the corner of his thin-lipped mouth, to twist it into a perpetual, ugly sneer.

'Keep an eye peeled, kid,' he told Pete, as

he poured his cup half full of coffee and filled it from a flat quart flask of almost colourless moonshine corn liquor, 'for any horsebacker that might top the ridge. I got word at the whisky peddler's last night that Zee Dunbar's wagon is camped at the head of the breaks. We better get these sleeper-marked calves branded before ol' Zee leads his men on circle to work the river bottom.'

Pete Craven would be the same stature as his father in a few more years. A five-foot-eight youth at eighteen, slim, long muscled, lean jawed, with a quick, lithe way of moving. His hair was darker than his sire's, almost black, until the sunlight gave it a reddish sheen. Pete's eyes were more grey than green, set wide apart under straight, black brows. He was a good hand with a green bronc, a better roper than the average seasoned cowhand. A quiet sort of kid who never spoke out of turn; too close-mouthed, perhaps, due to Booger Red's strict training. Pete had good cause to live in fear of his father, and whatever love and respect he was born with had long since been beaten out of him until a feeling akin to hatred, born of fear, had taken its place.

When Booger Red finished drinking his spiked coffee he swung into his saddle, shaking a loop into his catch-rope as he rode at a running walk towards the bunched calves at the far end of the corral. He was one of the best ropers in that part of the Montana cow country. He could have heeled the big calf he hazed from the bunch, picking up both hind legs with a sure loop, to make it easy for Pete. But instead he dropped the loop over its head and pulled the bawling, fighting calf across the corral to the branding fire by the saddle horn.

Pete went down the taut rope, his hogging-string between his teeth, and grabbed the calf's head and flank, and lifted the animal quickly. He hogtied it with sure, deft speed and jerked off the catch-rope, then opened the big blade of his jack-knife.

Booger Red sat his horse, coiling his rope, while he watched Pete change the Bradded Z earmark into his Boxed X earmark. Pete altered the right-ear crop to a swallow-fork with a single slice then the small under-bit notch on the left ear to a deep underslope that sliced off the lower part of the ear. Then Pete castrated the bull calf, and, selecting a bar iron heated to cherry red, he branded the calf in the Craven Boxed X iron. He jerked off the hogging-string and tailed up the calf, and the iron was back in the fire when Booger Red heeled the next calf and dragged it to the branding fire.

He had dragged up his seventh calf when

Zee Dunbar and two other horsebackers rode up. They had come quietly along the river instead of topping the ridge Pete was supposed to watch.

'Looks like you're short-handed, Booger Red.' Zee Dunbar rode alongside the corral and looked over. 'Always glad to lend a neighbour a hand at brandin' time.' The grin on his leathery face left his pale, grey eyes as cold as winter ice.

'Where the hell did you come from?' Booger Red's big hair-tufted hand dropped to the black butt of his holstered six-shooter.

'I've been waiting to pay you this visit.' Zee Dunbar's voice had a brittle sound. 'Better take a look at the two men with me, Booger Red, before you make any wrong move with your gun. I just hired these two hands who drifted up from Johnson County in Wyoming where there's a range war going on. Feller named Teal and his side pardner, Lance Rader. From what I hear, these two have built up tough reps in Wyoming.'

Booger Red cut a quick look at the two men. One was tall and lean, with black hair and beady, black eyes, a bone-handled six-shooter held almost carelessly in his hand. The other man was a range dude, from his black alligator boots and silver-mounted spurs to the crown of his new wide-brimmed, high-

4

crowned black Stetson hat. A handsome man, until you got a look at the thin-lipped mouth and pale-yellow eyes. He had an arrogant smile, a swagger to his well-muscled shoulders.

Booger Red's scarred mouth twisted sideways and his face was mottled, ugly, as his hand slid away from his gun.

'Drag up those newly-branded calves, Booger Red.' Zee Dunbar spoke, his voice quiet and deadly. 'Run a bar through your Boxed X and put them in the Bradded Z brand. When you and your whelp Pete get the job done, me and you is going to have a medicine talk.'

Zee Dunbar stepped from his saddle on to the corral and climbed down on the inside. He picked up Booger Red's cup and filled it with coffee. Zee was a short, heavy-set, compactly built man with sandy hair and a sunburnt complexion. A blunt-jawed man with cold, pale eyes. He stood there on his saddle-warped legs, watching Booger Red deftly rope and drag up a bawling calf to the fire.

'The best damned heeler in Montana,' Zee Dunbar said as he looked up into Booger Red Craven's bloodshot eyes, 'locked up in a two-by-four cell making horsehair bridles.'

Booger Red's thin-lipped mouth twitched sideways. He spat a stream of tobacco juice in the heavy dust between Zee's spurred, booted feet.

Pete straddled the calf, watching his father out of the corner of his eye as he wrapped the hogging-string to tie the calf's legs. The boy had often listened to his old man's bragging; how, if ever he was caught rustling cattle, no son of a bitch on earth could ever take him without a gun fight. But Booger Red's six-shooter was still in its holster tied down along his thigh.

Pete freed the loop from the calf's hind legs and stamped a bar through the fresh brand to vent it, then made a neat Bradded Z with the same iron before it had a chance to cool.

'The kid's a sure enough brand artist.' It was the range dude who spoke as he opened the corral gate and came through.

Pete stared at Lance Rader with a boy's frank admiration. Never before had he seen a man garbed in such fancy trimmings. As he came closer, Pete got the faint odour of bay rum he used on his hair and face after shaving.

Booger Red almost rode him down as he dragged up his next calf in a swirl of heavy dust.

'You pick this purty thing from a mail order catalogue, Zee?' Booger Red spat a stream of brown spittle at the polished alligator boots as he passed. 'Or did you find him in some sportin' house?'

'Count the notches on that white-handled gun he packs, Booger Red, then ask Lance Rader where he came from.' Zee grinned mirthlessly.

'Rassle that calf down,' Booger Red snarled at Pete.

Pete straddled the calf and tied him, hot resentment and mingled fear sickening him. As he freed the loop, Booger Red flicked the rope with its knotted hondo into Pete's face as he rode off. Pete crouched there, a small trickle of blood coming from both nostrils. Then he got to his feet, wiping the back of his dirty hand across his mouth, feeling the humiliation and shame of his cowardice, trying to keep it from showing. Fear of his father had been there since the beginning of his memory, the harsh, brutal sound of the man's voice, the quirtings from the shot-loaded rawhide quirt that hung from a wooden peg inside the kitchen of the log cabin which was their home. The scars healed over in a few days, but the contempt in Booger Red's eyes was there to stay, to torture him even in the oblivion of sleep.

Booger Red dragged up the last unbranded calf. 'This one will finish the job,' he said, draining the flask and throwing it over the corral as Pete branded and turned loose the calf.

'Step down,' Zee Dunbar told Booger Red. He took a thick brown manila envelope from the pocket of his old, fringed leather chaps. He squatted on his boot heels and pulled out an official-looking printed document.

'I'm giving you one way out, Booger Red,' Zee said. 'I can send you to the pen for a long stretch and your boy Pete to the reform school till he comes of age, then to the Deer Lodge prison. I can do that, Booger Red.'

Booger Red stepped off his horse and loosened the saddle cinch. He stood there on spread legs, thumbing his old hat back from his sweat-matted shock of hair.

'Or I can sign that bill of sale to my Boxed X outfit,' Booger Red said, a cold glint in his eyes.

'Lock, stock and barrel,' Zee said flatly. 'And you quit the country.' He pulled a second envelope from his pocket, saying, 'This is an indictment charging you with cattle rustling. If ever you come back to Montana, this indictment will be served with a bench warrant reading "Dead or Alive."'

Zee Dunbar held a document in each hand, his mirthless grin leaving his eyes cold and calculating. 'Name it, Booger Red!'

'I'll sign the travel orders. Me'n my kid'll pull out.'

'Pete stays here. You travel alone when you leave.'

'The hell you say!' Booger Red cut a quick look at his son, who was pulling branding irons from the fire and laying them in a neat row on the ground to cool off. 'How come you're keepin' my kid?' There was suspicion in his voice. 'He been keepin' you posted?' he asked.

'You got another guess coming if you think your whelp sold you down the river, Booger Red,' Zee told him. 'I'm keeping the kid here to work out those colts he's stolen from the Bradded Z. Two to three good colts missing every fall on the mare round-up and you got 'em all. The kid's going to work out those colts at forty a month. Either he makes a hand or I send him to reform school.'

'You laid back, Dunbar, waited till I'd built up this outfit to where it's worth something, then you moved in and took it for nothin'.' A nerve twitched along the knife scar, pulling the corner of his mouth sideways in tiny jerks. 'Like you've taken other little greasy-sack outfits to build up your big Bradded Z spread.' Booger Red's bloodshot green eyes slivered.

'You killed Tom Jones and claimed his outfit. You sent Mitch Moran to the pen and stole his outfit in a law court. Catfish Smith was pushed off his ferry-boat one night while he was haulin' some Bradded Z cowhands and their saddle horses across the river. A few weeks later Catfish Smith's saloon and store and land and ferry-boat belonged to Zee Dunbar. It was auctioned off at a sheriff's sale and you were the only bidder. Old Man Trotter blew his brains out rather than die in the Deer Lodge pen. And you got his little outfit. Now you got mine to fill out the string of ranches along both sides of the big Missouri. You got 'em all by just sittin' back and playin' your cards close to your belly.'

The slivered eyes held Zee Dunbar silent. A sudden twitch puckered the ridged scar, pulling the mouth upward to bare large tobacco-stained teeth. The laugh that came from his twisted mouth had an ugly taunting sound.

'By hell, you shore knifed yourself in the back, Zee,' he said behind the laugh, 'when you hired this tinhorn range dude. If I was to shoot him down now I'd be doin' you a big favour.' His narrowed eyes swivelled to cut a meaning look at Lance Rader, then he said, 'I just remembered where I'd seen you before, Rader, but I wouldn't tell Zee if I was to hang for keepin' my mouth shut.' Booger Red's chuckle had a harsh sound as he led his saddle horse out through the corral gate.

'I'll sign that bill of sale at the cabin, Zee,' he said over his shoulder. 'Then I'll drift yonderly.'

Pete Craven had the notion that somehow his old man had come out ahead. He had caught the stricken look in the cowman's eyes and the greyish pallor that had come into his face, like he was sick from some obscure malady beyond cure. Zee was staring hard at Lance Rader as he followed Booger Red out the gate.

Teal had slid down the corral. 'Don't take Booger Red's whisky talk too serious, Zee,' he said to the cowman, smiling thinly.

Zee Dunbar eyed the Wyoming gun-slinger coldly. 'When I need your advice I'll pay for it, Teal,' he said gruffly, then turned his back on Teal and walked away.

Pete followed the cowman and his two hired gunmen over to the cabin, bringing the coffee-pot along.

Pete managed, in spite of Booger Red's slovenly habits, to keep their cabin clean inside and out. In the lean-to shed the wood was neatly stacked and the dirt floor swept. Pete got a bottle of ink and a pen from a cupboard and put them on the table. Booger Red dipped the pen in the ink and signed where Zee Dunbar's blunt forefinger indicated the dotted line, then dropped the pen on the table. Zee picked it up and said curtly, 'Sign here as witness, kid. Teal and Rader can sign as witnesses after you.'

Booger Red took the quirt from its peg by the door, hooking two fingers through the loop and swinging it carelessly. Then with a swift vicious back-hand movement of arm and wrist, he slashed it across Pete's face just as the boy was putting the pot on the stove to heat the coffee.

Pete grit his teeth to hold back the outcry of pain, swaying a little as drops of blood beaded the raw welt. He watched Booger Red hang the loaded quirt back on the wooden peg and walk across the room to the short hallway leading to his room.

None of the three men in the cabin said anything or made the slightest motion to interfere. The uneasy silence held while they watched Booger Red Craven come back into the room, his bedroll over one shoulder. He opened a cupboard, hooked a forefinger through the handle of a fat brown jug of corn liquor and went out the door without a word.

Pete filled the battered tin basin and washed the blood from his face and hands. He dried off on a clean roller towel, his back to the three men. He watched through the open door while Booger Red threw his tarp-covered bed on one of his string of top cow horses, then roped it on with a one-man squaw-hitch. The bed horse packed, he shoved his Winchester carbine into the saddle scabbard and mounted his roan gelding. Leading his bed horse he rode down the trail towards the river, tall in the saddle, without a backward glance, south.

Pete turned around slowly, a thin trickle of blood along his cheek, his face pale under the tanned skin. He faced the three men.

Lance Rader was standing at a window, a 30–30 Winchester carbine in his hand. Teal stood at another window, his saddle gun in the crook of his arm. Zee Dunbar held a cup of hot coffee in both hands, his eyes fixed on Pete with a cold, calculating stare.

There was no doubt in Pete Craven's mind that Zee's hired killers had been ready to shoot Booger Red down if he had given them provocation.

'Saddle up, kid,' Zee Dunbar said. 'I'm takin' you to town. Anything you want to take along to that reform school, you better take now. You ain't a-comin' back.'

Pete Craven clenched his hands till his knuckles showed bone white, his teeth clamped till his jaw muscles ached.

'You said you'd let me work out the colts I stole. I don't want to go to reform school. I'll work for my grub...' Pete clamped his teeth down as he read the look in the cowman's hard eyes.

'You had to hire a couple of gunmen to side you,' Pete blurted out. 'You didn't have the guts to tackle Booger Red alone. It took three of you to get the job done.'

Zee tossed his empty cup into the dishpan on the back of the stove.

'You two fellers hang around in case Booger Red takes a notion to come back. Stay here till you hear from me. It might take me a few days to send the kid over the road.'

Riding away a few minutes later with Zee Dunbar, Pete, like Booger Red, never looked back.

This little ranch on the north bank of the Missouri River was the only home Pete had ever known. His mother had died before they had come here, before Pete had any memory of her. He had helped his father build the log cabin and barn and pole corrals. He had helped build up what he was leaving behind and there should have been pangs of regret as he rode off. But he felt none. Since he was old enough and big enough, Pete had planned on running away. He'd stayed awake nights planning his escape from the ranch, from Booger Red's drunken brutality. But somehow his plans had fallen through each time, because he dreaded the punishment Booger Red might inflict when he overhauled him and brought him back.

It was only when he was alone at the ranch that he found any measure of happiness and contentment there. Then he would lose himself in a sort of day-dream world. He'd swim over to Trapper's Island and prowl it aimlessly, or lie on a brush-hidden sandbar and listen to the river sounds. Cheated out of his boyhood and the companionship of early youth, Pete had grown up with a rare understanding of nature and things close to the earth and sky.

Winters, when the wide Missouri River froze over and the days were short, there was little time to be alone. The authorities had told Booger Red to send his son to school at Catfish Crossing or he'd be taken away by law. Pete had had to get up long before daylight to do the chores, and when school was out he had to get back to attend the ranch work before nightfall. There had been no time to play, no time to make friends with the other schoolchildren. Booger Red had beaten it into him to keep his mouth shut and tend to his own affairs, so that his reticence was misleading, misconstrued for sullenness by the other children. But Old Brocky, the schoolteacher, who ran the trading store and ferry-boat at Catfish Crossing knew better.

Old Brocky would write the lessons on the

blackboard in the little log cabin schoolhouse, then go back to his store. While the rest of the class talked and played games, Pete studied his books. He read everything he could get his hands on and last winter Old Brocky had confessed there wasn't anything more he could teach him.

'A stretch in the reform school,' Zee Dunbar broke the silence between them, 'will straighten you out, kid. I'm sendin' you there for your own good.' Zee twisted his head to look at the boy from under the low-pulled brim of his battered old hat as he whittled tobacco into his pipe. He struck a match across his old shotgun chaps and cupping the match flame in a gnarled hand, he puffed till his face was half hidden in tobacco smoke.

'You got the notion ol' Zee Dunbar is a prime son of a bitch, as bad or worse than Booger Red.' A slow grin spread the cowman's leathery face as he puffed thick clouds of smoke. 'That right, boy?' he asked.

'All I know is that I'd rather die than go to reform school,' Pete said.

'Supposin' I left you at the ranch like I told Booger Red, to work out the colts he made you steal. One of these times your old man would show up and he'd kill you, because he's got the notion you talked too much and are responsible for his being caught.'

Zee knocked the ashes from his pipe and reamed the bowl out with his knife before he spoke again.

'You make a hand at the reform school and I'll get you paroled,' he said. 'It'll either straighten the kinks outa you or send you to the Deer Lodge pen to finish your stretch when you come of age. It's strictly up to you, kid. No use in your swellin' up like a buck Injun, kid. It's for your own good. You'd a wound up in the pen if you trailed with Booger Red, or some gent with a law badge would have cut you down.'

Pete untangled a witch's knot in his horse's mane as he rode along in silence, his lips pulled in a tight line. The quirt had left a raw welt along his cheek and the blood had dried to form an uneven blotch on his lean jaw.

'You heard what Booger Red had to say about my getting hold of some little ranches along the Missouri River.' Zee tackled the subject from another angle. 'You better listen to my side of it before you get set in any opinion.' Zee eyed the boy narrowly as he talked.

'I rode up on Tom Jones while he was butcherin' a beef inside his horse corral. When Tom went for his gun I beat him to it. My Bradded Z brand was on the animal's hide and I found some steers with my brand worked into Jones's Rail 7. So I claimed his Seven Mile ranch and a court order deeded me the place. I made a winter line camp outa it.' Zee ran a wire through his pipe stem.

'Mitch Moran had done time before for horse stealin'. A hard case if there ever was one. Me'n the stock inspector caught him with thirty odd of stolen horses with worked brands he was holdin' in a trap pasture behind his ranch. Mitch pleaded guilty and the Judge threw the book at him. He was a two-time loser, a hardened criminal in the eyes of the law. The court gave me Moran's CK ranch as a reward.' Zee blew through the cleared pipe stem and twisted it back into place.

'When Catfish Smith got drunk on his own moonshine and fell off his ferry-boat, it was good riddance. Nobody pushed him off. It was a rainy night and the boat slippery. He was ferryin' a couple of my cowhands across the river with their horses. All three were loaded to the eyebrows. They'd gotten drunk with Catfish at his saloon that afternoon. The cowboys were holdin' their horses and never knew Catfish had fallen overboard. I got the outfit at a sheriff's sale a month later in October. It was the first blizzard of the season and I was the only man with guts enough to go to the auction so I got it at my own rock-bottom bid.' Zee Dunbar eyed Pete as he refilled and lit his pipe.

'Old Man Trotter,' Zee shook his head from side to side, 'everybody knew he was butcherin' my beef, which he called "Slow Elk." I told him it was all right if he was hungry and needed meat, but when he started peddlin' my beef to a bootleg butcher at Landusky, that was carryin' things too far. Old Man Trotter used one of his own T UP and T DOWN hides with every Bradded Z beef he delivered at night to the Landusky butcher. He kept the old hide soaked in the river to keep it from dryin' out between trips. That year-old hide got to where it stunk so bad it smelled up the town every time he came in. The damned ol' fool would get drunk on the money and brag about it around the saloons. But I made no move to stop him until a new stock inspector, out to make a rep for himself, threw Old Man Trotter in jail and arrested the butcher. He subpoenaed me to testify but I refused to prosecute. The old man had come up the trail from Texas with my dad with the XIT trail herd of longhorns and that's how come I never would charge him with butcherin' my beef.

'It wasn't long after that he got on a hell of a drunk and claimed there were snakes rattlin' inside his skull. He shoved the barrel of his six-shooter in his ear and pulled the trigger to blast out the snake nest.' Zee Dunbar grinned faintly as he looked at Pete.

'I reckon that about takes care of what Booger Red said against me,' he finished.

Pete's beardless face never changed expression. He had missed no word of the cowman's story, wondering if Zee was leading up to something that concerned him, but whatever the cowman had in mind he kept it to himself. He wanted young Pete Craven to think things over. He had met every one of Booger Red's accusations with a plausible answer, a logical reason. By that time they were in sight of the Bradded Z home ranch. A cluster of log cabins and cattle shed and pole corrals stood along the banks of Rock Creek. A big two-storied house was apart from the smaller log cabins that were the bunkhouse and cook-house, blacksmith shop and the buggy shed. The ranch looked like a small village with the pine-timbered slopes of the Little Rockies in the background.

The cowman's pride of ownership and the power that went with a big cow outfit showed in his face and the gleam in his pale eyes when he said, 'Best damn ranch in the country. The main house has town plumbin' with two bathtubs; a hot air, coal-burnin' furnace, and furnished with the best money could buy. The wife has a hired girl to do the cookin' and housework. She don't have to lift a broom or dustrag.'

Zee Dunbar sat square in the saddle, his weight divided equally in both stirrups. He had a habit of leaning forward across the saddle horn, an almost round-shouldered look, with his thick muscled neck, the blunt jaw jutting. There was a brooding shadow in his cold eyes. It was as if he'd forgotten young Pete when he spoke, riding a little ahead of the boy and not knowing it.

'I've given Tracy everything she's ever asked for and still she's never satisfied ... first it was two beds, then it was separate rooms. She couldn't stand my snorin' and the smell of barn and horse sweat. Gawdamighty, it beats the stink of that French perfume and cologne she uses. Hates the ranch because it's too lonesome. Wants to winter in Butte where the sulphur smoke from the smelters has killed off the trees and grass; has a three-storied house picked out for herself and me tied down here; thinks I can hire a foreman to ramrod a big spread like the Bradded Z; says she's too young to be cut off from the city lights, snowed in on a God-forsaken cow ranch. It took a trainload of four-year-old native steers that fetched top price at the Union Stockyards at Chicago to buy her the diamonds she wears. A hell of a note when she can't stand the stink of a little cow manure on a man's boots.'

Zee Dunbar clamped his teeth down and reined up a little. 'Hell, I been talkin' out loud, boy.' Zee forced a grin. 'But I reckon you heard nothin' but what the whole damn cow country already knows. They say nobody but a damned old fool would marry a girl young enough to be his daughter. Makes me the laughin' stock of the country. That right, boy?' he asked.

Pete Craven felt uncomfortable under the cowman's brooding stare, the bitterness of his forced grin.

'It ain't for me to say,' Pete said finally.

'Booger Red was laughin' up his sleeve when he rode off, and I know why. I know where he'd seen that range dude before. At a dance in Landusky. I was laid up at the ranch and Lance Rader took my wife to the dance in my red-wheeled top buggy, drivin' my trottin' team.'

As they rode down the low ridge to the ranch Zee straightened up in the saddle. His young wife had come out on the wide porch to wave a greeting, and Pete got his first look at the woman Zee had been talking about. What he saw was a tall slender girl with tanned skin, her sleek black hair parted in the middle and plaited in two heavy braids that hung below her slim waist. She wore a sleeveless blue cotton dress and low-heeled slippers, her legs bare and tanned. The only jewelry she wore was a plain wedding ring. Her white teeth showed as she smiled, blowing a kiss with both hands as the cowman made a half awkward motion of his arm to return the greeting.

The two men dismounted in front of the barn. Zee said as they unsaddled, 'Purty, eh, boy? She's got a way with men, all the way from kids your age to damned grey-headed fools like me. You're bound to like Tracy.'

CHAPTER TWO

'Whew!' Tracy Dunbar gasped, her laugh soft as she freed herself from the strong embrace of her cowman husband. 'I swear you cracked some ribs, Zee. Who's the handsome cowboy you've brought home?'

'Young Pete Craven. Booger Red's boy. I've taken over Craven's Boxed X greasy-sack outfit, and claimed the kid,' Zee explained.

Zee's wife held out her hand and Pete felt the vibrant warmth of the slim fingers gripping his callused hand. Still holding his hand, the fingertips of her left hand traced the raw welt along his cheek. 'Who did this to you, Pete?' she asked. 'Was it Zee?'

'No, ma'am.' Pete's voice stuck in his throat and came with dry uneven sound. 'It was my old man. It's nothing.'

'There's a lot of dirt and dried blood there. I'll clean it up before infection sets in,' Tracy said, letting go the boy's hand. She turned and gave Zee a searching look. 'What happens to Pete, Zee?' she asked.

'We caught Booger Red and the kid branding some weaned calves in my earmark. I gave Booger Red his choice of signin' his outfit over to me and quittin' the country or goin' to the pen for a long stretch. He quit the country.' Zee shrugged his shoulders. 'What happens to Pete will depend on Judge Dewar at Chinook. Like as not he'll send him to reform school till he comes of age.'

'You'd send this boy to reform school, Zee?' Tracy's voice sounded tense.

'It's out of my hands, once I turn him over to the law. It's strictly up to Judge Dewar, Tracy.'

'Don't lie to me, Zee Dunbar.' She spoke in brittle tones. 'You can have him paroled if you want to. All you have to do is to sign a paper stating you'll be responsible for him.'

'I got no time to ride herd on a kid that's been taught every trick of cattle rustlin' and horse stealin',' Zee growled.

'You drove Booger Red out of the country. You got his outfit. You can drop the charges against this boy if you've a mind to.' The blood had drained from Tracy's face, leaving it pale beneath the coating of tan. Her grey-green eyes glinted as she stood erect, her small breasts outlined against the fabric of her dress. 'Give the boy a chance, Zee,' she pleaded.

The eyes of the grizzled cowman and his young wife met and held for a long time. It was Zee who finally looked away. He shrugged his heavy shoulders, a grin forcing itself across the leathery face as he looked at Pete Craven.

'Anytime a married man tells you, kid,' Zee said, his hard lips twisting crookedly, 'he's the boss, look out for him. He'll lie about somethin' else.' He turned away and walked down the hallway, his spur rowels jingling with each bow-legged stride.

'There's a lot of mail piled up on your desk in the den, Zee,' Tracy called after him. 'One from the Indian Department is marked urgent.'

Zee grunted, swearing under his breath as he opened a door at the end of the hall and slammed it behind him.

Pete Craven stood there in awkward silence, the blood pounding into his throat.

'You aren't used,' Tracy came closer, smiling, her eyes soft, 'to anybody taking your part.'

'No, ma'am,' Pete blurted. 'That's the first time...'

'There's always a first time,' she said, her eyes on a level with his, 'for everything, Pete. Don't try to thank me, get that cut patched up right now.' She led him to a bathroom.

'This is Zee's bathroom,' she explained. 'Wash up while I get some medicine.'

Pete rolled up his sleeves. His head and face were down close to the wash bowl filled with hot water when he heard the jingle of spurs and Zee's harsh voice.

'A man no sooner turns his back than he gets a damn knife in his gizzard. That rep I had workin' with the ID wagon got into a ruckus. I got to get to the sub-agency right away. You stay here till I get back, Pete. There's always an extra bedroll in the bunkhouse. Promise me you won't run off, kid.'

'I won't run off,' Pete said, drying his face on a rough towel.

'I'll be back sometime tomorrow. There's plenty of chores around the barn to keep you busy. See that you get them done.'

Zee stomped down the hall and the front door slammed behind him.

Tracy's low throaty laugh sent vibrations through the eighteen-year-old Pete, making his pulse pound up into his throat.

She came into the bathroom and poured iodine on some cotton. Standing close to Pete, she slid the cotton swab along the raw welt with one deft sure move. 'I know that hurts,' she said, her voice soft as silk. She tossed the used cotton into a waste-basket and wiped a brown stain on her fingers on the end of a towel, smiling a little.

'Like music, Pete?' she asked as they left the bathroom.

'Yes, ma'am.'

'My name's Tracy. Come along, I've got a stack of records. You can play them while I get supper. The hired girl quit. Too lonesome here on the ranch, she told me, and she got no argument there.' Tracy led the way into the parlour with its flowered Brussels carpet and heavy dark oak chairs and sofa. She cranked the Victor phonograph.

Pete eyed the shiny ornate phonograph with its huge pink morning-glory horn. It was the first of its kind he had ever seen and it filled him with a sort of breathless awe.

Tracy beckoned him closer, saying, 'It won't bite. I'll show you how it works.' She screwed in a needle and selected a record played by Sousa's Band, watching the changing expression on Pete's face.

She showed him how to fix the needle, wind the crank and set the needle on the outer edge of the record, her fingers on his, guiding his hand. 'Play what records you want while I get supper on the table.' She rumpled his thick wiry black hair and kissed him lightly on the cheek.

Pete relaxed slowly like a tight wound spring of a clock unwinds with each ticking. He was enjoying himself more than he had taken pleasure in anything in his life. He forgot everything else in this marvellous absorption of the phonograph that was like a magic carpet transporting him to strange uncharted, unknown worlds. Now and then he caught a brief glimpse of Tracy as she came from the kitchen to look in on him and smile gaily, calling out something to bring a grin to Pete's face.

He tried not to look at the slim shapely bare legs, the thrust of her small breasts against her dress, but he could not help his quick, shy glances at her that quickened his pulse. Presently she called him to supper.

They ate in the kitchen at a small table. She piled his plate with thick slices of rare roast beef, mashed potatoes and gravy and canned peas. Hot biscuits and real butter and homemade strawberry jam and pickles. Apple pie and chocolate cake for dessert. She rinsed the dishes and stacked them in the dishpan and they went back into the parlour to play more records.

'Have you ever learned to dance?' Tracy asked Pete as she put on the 'Blue Danube' waltz.

Pete shook his head, ill at ease now.

'Then I'll be your first teacher.' The light gaiety of her laugh was a little forced as she came close to him. 'Put your right arm around my waist,' she instructed, holding his left hand in hers, her other arm across his shoulders. 'Don't be stiff-backed. Hold me closer. I won't break in two. Now, relax. I'll lead. Let your feet follow mine.'

For a time it was clumsy and awkward and Pete was red-faced, with beads of nervous perspiration breaking out to add to his discomfort. His knees felt shaky and his legs weak as the record played itself out. They paused while Tracy rewound the phonograph and put on another record. Pete mopped the sweat from his face with a soggy bandana.

'You're doing fine for a beginner.' She moved close to him. 'Forget about the footwork and let the music get inside you, get the feel of its rhythm and forget the mechanics of dancing. I'm enjoying it.' She laughed shortly as she led off, her cheek against his, the perfume of her hair heady as strong wine. Pete had lost a lot of that self-conscious embarrassment by the time the record played out.

They sat side by side on the sofa and played more music until the big clock on the mantel struck twelve.

'I'd better be getting over to the bunkhouse,' Pete said.

'You can sleep in Zee's room,' Tracy said. 'I'm afraid to stay here alone at night.' She got up and lit a candle in a short silver candlestick.

Turning out the lamp and holding the candle high she led the way up the broad stairs. The bedroom doors stood ajar on either side of the hall. She led him into Zee's room and lit the lamp from the candle and adjusted the wick, then turned down the covers on the big brass bed and laid out one of her husband's nightshirts.

When she had left the room Pete sat on the edge of the bed and pulled off his boots and undressed. He put on the white nightshirt and eyed himself in the large mirror over the dresser. He had never before worn a nightshirt nor slept between sheets, and was scowling at his image in the mirror when he heard Tracy say outside the closed door:

'I'm finished in the bathroom at the end of

the hall if you feel like a hot bath to take the ache out of your dancing muscles. Don't be bashful about using things. Zee sometimes soaks in the tub till he falls asleep.'

Back in his room after a bath, he raised the window blinds and a shaft of moonlight came in the open window. He crawled between the white sheets. He closed his eyes and lay there, strangely disturbed by all that had happened to him since dawn, wondering what tomorrow would be, until a relaxed drowsiness swept over him. He was almost asleep when the whisper of Tracy's voice seemed to creep into his half dreams of her.

'Pete . . . are you awake?' Her whisper was close to him. 'I'm scared, Pete. . . I couldn't get to sleep. I kept worrying about you. What Zee has planned for you. Zee can be cold-blooded and merciless when he goes after something and nothing can stop him.'

Pete heard and felt the faint creak of the bed-springs as Tracy sat on the edge of the bed. Then suddenly he heard the sound of a horse's shod hoofs, the creak of saddle leather, through the open window.

Tracy was off the bed and saying, 'Quick, Pete. Get up and wait right here.' She disappeared in the darkness.

Pete heard the pounding on the front door.

'Take this,' Tracy whispered, as she came

back into the room to stand close to him.

Pete felt the hard cold butt of a .38 Smith & Wesson hammerless revolver Tracy shoved into his hand.

'If that's Zee come sneaking back to catch us, he'll kill you, Pete. And God knows what he'll do to me. Get downstairs quickly, and shoot first and don't miss.'

Her fingers bit into his arm.

Pete had just reached the bottom step when the front door burst open.

A big hulk of a man, too tall and long legged to be Zee Dunbar stood half crouched in the doorway, the moonlight behind him.

'Show a light, kid!' A rasping voice sounded. 'You wasn't at the bunkhouse where Zee Dunbar said you'd be, so by Gawd, you must be in here. Strike a match. I'm takin' no chances with Booger Red's whelp.'

Pete crouched behind the big wooden newel post, a tight grip on the gun Tracy had given him. His mouth and throat felt dry and cold sweat slicked his gun hand, but there was no time to be afraid in those tense split seconds.

'I'm comin' in after you, kid, and Gawd help you when I drag you outa your hole. I got a bench warrant to pick you up and take you to jail.'

The big bulk shuffled forward, boot heels scraping, spur rowels clanking, the moonlight silhouetting the large frame. Pete saw the six-shooter in his hand tilt and heard the double click of the gun hammer thumbed back.

Then the big .45 Colt spewed a heavy slug that hit the newel post, so close to Pete's head he felt the splinters. The man's cursing could be heard above the gun echoes.

Pete waited a few seconds, then as the man lurched towards him Pete jerked the trigger without knowing it. The big bulk sagged and fell with a heavy crash on the carpet.

'Pete!' Tracy's tight voice sounded from the head of the stairs, 'Are you hurt, Pete?'

'I'm all right,' Pete answered.

Tracy appeared now with a lighted candle and shielded the flickering flame in her hand as she came down the stairs slowly. She had a dark red-quilted robe over her nightgown, slippers on her bare feet.

'Get his gun, Pete,' she said, as she closed the front door.

Pete picked up the long-barrelled six-shooter from the floor a few feet away from the dead man. As he straightened up he saw the nickel-plated law badge pinned to the man's open vest. The blood drained from his face and shock gripped him, chilling his belly.

Tracy lit the lamp in the front parlour. 'Don't stand there, Pete,' she called out, her voice brittle, 'staring at that thing.

Come in here.'

His gait was a little unsteady as he went into the lighted parlour.

Tracy stood at a side table, pouring whisky from a cut-glass decanter into two water tumblers. She shoved a filled glass into Pete's hand, saying, 'Drink it down, Pete.'

'You know who it was?' she asked, taking a large swallow from her glass.

Pete drank the raw whisky and shook his head slowly.

'He was Big Jim West, Deputy Sheriff at Landusky. He needed killing, Pete. Everyone knows he was no good.'

'All I know,' Pete said in a toneless voice, 'I killed him. I killed a man with a law badge and they'll hang me.'

They did not know that the front door had opened and Lance Rader had come in, until he suddenly appeared in the doorway.

His high-crowned hat was pushed back as he stood on widespread legs, his pants shoved, Texas style, into his boot tops.

'Looks like Big Jim West busted up quite a party,' Rader said as he crossed the room and took the decanter of whisky from Tracy Dunbar's hand and splashed some into a glass and drank it down.

'What brought you here?' Tracy asked, white lipped.

'I figured Zee was on his way to Chinook with Booger Red's kid, so I came to keep you from gettin' lonely till Zee got back.' Lance Rader poured himself another drink and downed it. His yellow eyes had an ugly muddy look when he looked at Pete and said, 'Looks like you cut the big gut, kid. I'm takin' you to jail.'

'No.' Tracy spoke tensely, her hands clenched. 'Let Pete alone. I gave him the gun Zee gave me and he killed Big Jim West when he broke in and started shooting. Pete shot in self-defense and if he wants to stay and stand trial I'll clear him on the witness stand. But he is going to get his chance to quit the country, and you aren't going to stop him.'

Lance Rader smiled thinly with twisted lips. 'Maybe Pete Craven would be safer in jail than he'd be on the dodge,' he said.

'What are you trying to say?' Tracy asked.

'I don't reckon ol' Zee would like the looks of this setup; Pete Craven wearin' his nightshirt and drinkin' his likker, instead of bunkin' down in the bunkhouse. If the kid runs for it now, Zee Dunbar will follow him to hell and back and kill that young Pistol Pete where he cuts his sign. And damn well you know it, lady.'

'He slept in Zee's bed,' Tracy said, 'because I was afraid to stay here alone. Zee hasn't the dirty filthy mind you have, mister.'

'Zee Dunbar's in his fifties, married to a twenty-year-old girl. Naturally he's bound to be jealous of any younger man you ask to spend the night in your house, with him away.' The yellow eyes were shrewd and cunning as he looked past the girl to Pete.

Pete Craven felt empty and cold, sick inside, but his eyes never flinched from the probing look in Lance Rader's eyes.

'Any man,' Pete spoke in a dry terse voice, 'you or Zee Dunbar or any man on earth, says what you're thinkin' right now, is a dirty liar.'

'Where'd you get the guts to speak up, kid? From Zee's likker?' Lance asked. 'I was there when your old man quirted you and you never raised a hand,' he added.

'I've been scared of Booger Red since I can remember,' Pete said slowly. 'But I'm not scared of you or Zee Dunbar. I killed a man. I'm going to stand trial. I got no notion of runnin' away, but I don't need you to take me in. I got it made to give myself up to Sheriff Ike Niber at Chinook.'

'You're supposed to be at the Craven place thirty miles from here, Lance Rader,' Tracy cut in, her voice cold. 'If I tell Zee Dunbar why you came here, that fancy gun you carry won't do you much good. Zee will kill you and you know it, so you better get the hell out of his house and back where you belong.'

'You aim to tell Zee I came here tonight?' Rader asked.

'Not unless he asks me.'

'What about you, kid?' Lance Rader's hand was on the notched butt of his gun.

'I'll keep my mouth shut. But if Zee wants to know if you were here, I won't lie about it.'

Lance Rader helped himself to another big drink. 'You two talk outa turn and I'll tell Zee a story that's one for the book.' Lance grinned as he turned away and walked into the hall. 'You keep your mouth shut, kid, and some day I'll whittle you out a leather medal for killin' Big Jim West,' Lance said, as he went out and banged the door shut.

'I'm to blame, Pete,' Tracy said, her voice brittle.

Pete straightened his drooped shoulders and turned to face her, a scared look in his eyes. 'You better telephone Landusky and get Zee here,' Pete told her.

'The 'phone line has been down since yesterday. And anyhow, Zee Dunbar is the last person I want here.' Tracy put both hands on Pete's shoulders, her fingers digging in desperately. 'Your best bet is to make a getaway. I'll cover your trail, Pete.' Her narrowed eyes looked green. 'That dead man has a law badge pinned on his vest and they'll make it tough on you, no matter if it was a justified killing. You'd better quit the country till the stink dies down.'

'I'm not runnin' away from it,' Pete repeated stubbornly. 'I'm stayin' right here till somebody shows up.'

'Well then,' Tracy's voice was a harsh conspiratorial whisper, 'we'll load Big West's carcass in the push cart at the barn and dump it in the bunkhouse. We'll say that you were asleep in there when he busted in with a bench warrant and a six-shooter. He fired the first shot and kept shooting until you killed him. You can take his gun and shoot holes in the bunkhouse. There's nobody around to listen. I'll clean the blood off the hall carpet and fix the door lock. You killed Big Jim West at the bunkhouse, understand?'

A cold shiver wired down Pete's spine as he saw the hard green glitter in Tracy's eyes as her fingers dug into his shoulders. She read the look in his eyes.

'Listen, kid,' she said. 'If Zee finds out the facts he'll twist them around to suit his own jealous notions. He'll kill you and me too. Lance Rader told the truth. Nobody in the cow country would believe any different. They'd agree that Zee Dunbar was more than justified in killing you. Have you ever heard of the Unwritten Law, kid?' she asked, her eyes narrowed as she watched the expression on his face.

The loud clanging of the telephone bell in the hallway broke them apart as if a gun blasted the silence of the big house.

'That's Zee,' Tracy said, putting down the empty glass and wiping her mouth with the back of a trembling hand. 'I can tell by the way he never lets up. He's so mule-headed he'll keep it up till daylight so I might as well answer it.' She gave Pete a bitter sardonic twisted smile as a look of cunning crept into her eyes.

Pete watched her as she stepped around the ugly big bulk of the dead man to the wall telephone and lifted the receiver. Every word that left her lips came to him as he stood motionless, his legs braced.

'I've been trying to get Landusky for an hour, Zee,' Tracy was saying. 'The line's been down ... Yes, Deputy Sheriff West was here ... He's still here ... No, he can't come to the 'phone ... Why? Because he's dead ... That's right. Dead ... You want me to spell it out for you ... Don't shout in my ear, Zee ... No, I didn't kill the big drunken badge polisher ... Young Pete Craven shot him ... The kid was asleep in the bunkhouse ... West brought him to the house ... wanted to use the telephone to call you ... busted the doorlock and came in just as I came down the stairs ... I had that little gun you gave me and the kid grabbed it out of my hand while West was cranking the 'phone bell. Big West shot first and missed the kid, who was behind the big bannister post at the foot of the stairs. He kept shooting till the kid shot him and the gunfight was over.

'You're breaking my eardrum with your shouting, Zee ... What? ... Yes, the kid's here. Says he won't leave till you get here ... All right ... all right ... I'll keep him on ice till you get here ... the kid's handcuffed ...' Something of the natural colour had come back into Tracy's cheeks as she hung up.

'It takes a woman to think fast,' she said. 'Come here, Pete.'

Pete came into the shadowed hallway.

'Take Jim West's six-shooter and stand here by the 'phone,' she told Pete. 'Shoot a couple of bullets into the stairway. Better put another slug into the post. This is no time to get finicky. If you haven't the guts to shoot, I'll do it for you.'

Pete picked up the big Colt .45 as Tracy stepped in behind him. He put two slugs into the stair steps and one into the bannister post. Then Tracy took the smoking gun and fitted it into the big dead hand. She had the handcuffs in her hand when she straightened up.

'Hold out your hands,' she said. 'This'll add the finishing touch to the story we'll stick to.'

'I better get this nightshirt off,' Pete said, pulling it over his head.

Tracy laughed with a brittle sound as she snatched it and ran upstairs. She was back in a moment with his undershirt and shirt. She fastened the steel handcuffs on Pete's wrists. Her face was flushed and she was breathing quickly as she looked him over and nodded approval.

'Help yourself to a drink, Pete, you look green around the gills. I have to run up and put clean sheets on Zee's bed. You be thinking over what I told Zee on the telephone so we'll have an air-tight story with no loopholes.' She pushed past him into the parlour and filled a water tumbler with whisky and shoved it into Pete's manacled hands as he came in. She stayed until Pete had downed the raw whisky, then ran upstairs.

If he stuck to her fabricated lies, Pete Craven was in a tight spot. She'd said he'd grabbed her gun, thereby forcing the gunfight on the big law officer. He knew he didn't have a foot to stand on now that her lies had changed the entire picture. The insidious relaxation of the alcohol was already working on him before he thought about fighting against it, and the worry about having killed a man had perceptibly lessened from its first bitter stark realism.

Tracy had changed into a gingham house dress. Pete heard her say, 'It's in the bag, Pete, if we stick to our story. When I give my eyewitness testimony, you'll be free, kid, don't worry about that.' She poured more whisky and insisted on Pete drinking it.

Pete was asleep on the big horsehair couch when Zee Dunbar and Doctor Mayberry, the coroner, and six men they had gathered in town, rode up to the Bradded Z ranch at sunrise. Pete was dead drunk and passed out cold.

'I gave the kid some whisky to calm him down, Zee,' Tracy told her husband. 'I didn't realize he wasn't used to liquor. He was getting panicky and wild-eyed, talked about making a getaway before you got here.'

'I never thought the kid had guts enough to use a gun.' Zee Dunbar scowled down at the unconscious Pete. 'I can't figure it.'

'Pete didn't want to go to jail, Zee,' Tracy said. 'He'd worked himself into a desperate frame of mind and when he saw the gun in my hand, he took a frantic chance. All he wanted was to be free. If West hadn't pulled his gun and shot first, the kid would have been out the door and gone in the night.'

'The only thing this side of hell that'll keep

Pete Craven from stretchin' rope, is that he ain't of legal age,' Zee was saying as he walked into the hall where the coroner was examining the dead man.

CHAPTER THREE

The trial of Pete Craven was, according to the opinion of the morbidly curious crowd that packed the courtroom, a disappointing spectacle.

Those who had come to get a good look at Zee Dunbar's young wife were doomed to disappointment. Mrs. Zee Dunbar, the star witness, was too ill according to the doctor, to attend the trial. Her sworn deposition as the only eyewitness to the murder of Deputy Sheriff Jim West was read aloud by the prosecuting attorney.

Pete Craven had no money to hire a lawyer. Judge Dewar had the court appoint as his defence attorney an ageing, once brilliant criminal lawyer, named Stephen Costello. Whisky and gambling and women were the deadly triumvirate that had doomed one of the most spectacular criminal attorneys ever to plead and win a hopeless case in the Montana courts. Now Steve Costello earned a few dollars when, for old time's sake, Judge Dewar appointed him to defend a man too poor to hire his defence.

The day before the trial Steve Costello had somehow managed to get a copy of Tracy Dunbar's sworn deposition. He read it aloud to Pete Craven as he sat on his cell bunk.

Pete, from time to time, looked up at the tall lean attorney in a rusty black broadcloth suit that had once come from an expensive tailoring shop in Chicago; the frayed cuffs of a once fine white Irish linen custom-made shirt; the lean-jawed, hawk-beaked face with sunken bloodshot grey eyes shadowed under shaggy white brows; the thick white hair.

When he finished reading he tossed the clipped-together typewritten pages on the bunk.

His shadowed eyes looked down at Pete to fix the boy's stare. He said, 'Unless you deny this sworn deposition, Pete, you'll be looking through prison bars the best years of your life.'

Pete Craven sat there, his clenched hands between his knees. His face was pale and drawn, and there was a stricken look in his eyes as he clamped his jaws till the muscles quivered and ached in his stubborn silence.

'Chivalry in any man,' Steve Costello spoke softly, 'is a rare and precious quality, given to a chosen few. I once held that spotless white banner aloft, as I waited deep in slime and filth and muck that clayed my feet, even while my head was in the stars. God help me, I still have something of it that will always be retained.' He dropped a hand on Pete's shoulder.

'Your mind is made up, son,' he said gently. 'Who am I to dissuade you? Tomorrow morning we will enter a plea of guilty and your life will be at the mercy of the court. Amen and God help you, Pete Craven.'

The lawyer took a long black cheroot from his vest pocket and lit it. Then sat straddle of the straight-back chair facing the prisoner.

'You will not be forced to take the witness stand, to lie and perjure yourself in illicit collaboration of a woman's skillful lying to save her reputation.

'That young district attorney will misconstrue our plea of guilty as a token of defeat. He will bask in the light of easy victory. And so be it.' Steve Costello's eyes pierced the blue fog of cigar smoke. 'You will serve your time in the reform school and on your legal twenty-first birthday, when you become of legal age, I give you my word and promise that I will be in the warden's office with a writ that will renew this miscarriage of justice, to be tried in tomorrow's court.' Steve

Costello smiled faintly. 'How old are you, Pete?' he asked.

'Eighteen,' Pete said.

Steve Costello flicked the long ash from his cigar as his hand motioned towards the large cardboard box he had brought in and set down on the cement floor.

'I stopped at the store and got you a suit and a white shirt and necktie. I want you to appear decently clothed when you're in the courtroom. The general appearance of a prisoner counts more than anyone realizes. Polish your boots and scrub up, and look Judge Dewar in the eye when he tells you to stand to receive your sentence. That's all I ask, son.'

Pete eyed the cardboard box. 'Store clothes cost money, sir,' he said, shaking his head doubtfully.

'Let me worry about that,' said the lawyer. 'That's part of my job, like seeing to it that you get a haircut to-day and a decent supper.' Steve Costello got up, a smile on his lean face as he said, 'I've got to go now, but I'll drop in tomorrow morning to look you over.'

Pete Craven had a clean-cut boyish look as he sat in an armchair beside his attorney, dressed in a blue double-breasted suit, a white shirt and blue polka dot tie. Once he got over his stagefright as the packed courtroom eyed him, whispering, he settled back comfortably, his eyes searching the courtroom for a glimpse of Lance Rader. But the range dude wasn't among the men. Nor was Zee Dunbar.

A slow hour passed while the prosecuting attorney and Steve Costello, using a lot of legal terms, argued some questions before the grey-haired Judge Dewar.

Finally Steve Costello said in a sharp voice, 'My client pleads guilty, your Honour.'

Judge Dewar leaned forward to look at the accused prisoner as he nodded towards the jury box.

'The case involved will not need the services of you gentlemen of the jury,' he said. 'Pete Craven has entered a plea of guilty. Therefore, it is my duty as judge of this court to pass sentence.'

'Is there anything,' Judge Dewar looked down across the steel-rimmed eyeglasses at the prisoner, 'you would like to say in your own behalf, Pete Craven, before this court passes judgment?'

Pete Craven met the eyes of Judge Dewar unflinchingly as he got slowly to his feet. His whole being was numbed with an utter hopelessness that had robbed him of everything meant for courage and fortitude he stood so badly in need of at this crucial moment.

'No, sir,' Pete Craven said, trying to put bravery into the two short words.

Steve Costello rose to his feet, standing beside his young client.

'Your Honour,' he said, speaking to the judge as if the two men were alone. 'Pete Craven has been raised as a ranch kid, taught never to voice his opinion on his elders. He stands here, bewildered, confused, friendless and alone, but my arm across his shoulder feels no tremor of cowardice; there is no shifting fear in his eyes.'

Steve Costello took a step backward, as if he were leaving Pete Craven alone. His glance flicked the young prosecutor.

'My young and worthy opponent has won an easy victory, it seems, over an old broken-down has-been,' Costello said quietly. 'But, your Honour, before you pass sentence on this boy, I would beg five minutes of the court's time, if you would grant the favour.' The attorney took a cheap dollar Ingersoll watch from his vest pocket and laid it on the bare table in front of him.

Judge Dewar removed his spectacles, gesturing with them for Pete Craven to sit down. His smile touched the eyes of the dour Scot's face, putting a light into their stern depths. 'Proceed, counsel,' he said.

'Your Honour,' Steve Costello bowed

stiffly, 'gentlemen of the jury, ladies and gentlemen, I thank you.' He turned to sweep the courtroom with his shadowed eyes.

'There are certain discrepancies about this case that are, to put it as an understatement, puzzling.' Costello raised one hand and with his other hand he pulled down his forefinger.

'First: Young Pete Craven never owned a gun of any kind, nor carried one at any time. While the man he shot to death had killed five men, two of them before a law badge was pinned on him.' Steve Costello pulled down the next finger.

'Secondly: The reason my youthful client is without funds to hire a younger, more able attorney to defend him, is because Zee Dunbar, owner of the Bradded Z Ranch, has laid claim to the Craven Boxed X Ranch on the banks of the Missouri River, to add to his vast land holdings, robbing this boy of the only home he has ever known.

'Zee Dunbar and two hired gunmen, fresh from the Wyoming Cattle War in Johnson County's bloody feud, caught this boy's father, known as Booger Red Craven, branding some of Dunbar's calves, and under the threat of his hired guns, he made Booger Red Craven sign a bill of sale to the Boxed X Ranch over to him, then told him to quit the country.

'Zee Dunbar took Pete Craven into his protective custody, left the boy alone at the Bradded Z Ranch while he attended to other business in Landusky, which included getting a bench warrant sworn out for Pete Craven so that he could be picked up on the same calf-branding charge he'd used to send Booger Red out of the country.

'Those who had reason to know Deputy Sheriff Jim West, knew him for a man who drank heavily and was apt to get quarrelsome and belligerent in his cups; a quart a day man, they said of Jim West who was sent to arrest an unarmed, badly frightened boy who never packed a gun in his life.' Steve Costello's eyes glinted strangely as he looked around the room, then glanced at the dollar watch. He pulled down a third finger.

'Thirdly: the only eyewitness to the shooting of Deputy Sheriff Jim West was Zee Dunbar's wife. You all heard at the opening of this trial my young and worthy opponent say that Mrs. Zee Dunbar was too ill, on a statement from her doctor, to attend this trial. Her sworn deposition has been read and filed in the records of this court.' Steve Costello straightened his bent fingers and lowered his hand, a twisted bitter smile on his lips as he said, 'Yet Mrs. Zee Dunbar was seen, apparently in excellent health, boarding the westbound train at four-thirty this morning at Malta. The station agent said he sold her a ticket to Butte.' Steve Costello looked at his watch, then glanced at the clock on the wall as the hands stood exactly at twelve noon.

The ticking of the clock was the only sound that broke the silence as the defence attorney sat down. He gripped Pete's shoulder, smiling faintly at the tense, white-lipped boy.

Judge Dewar's wooden gavel sounded loudly as it shattered the hushed silence. He glanced up at the clock, and said, 'Court's recessed until one o'clock. Clear the court!'

Judge Dewar dismissed the prosecutor with a wave of the wooden gavel. He beckoned the defence attorney to him as he wiped his specs on a large white handkerchief.

'Sit tight, kid,' the sheriff in the chair beside Pete said. 'If I was the judge I'd turn you loose.'

'Hoist a chair up here, Ike,' Judge Dewar told Ike Niber, the sheriff. 'Bring young Pete Craven up. Pete and I have some things to talk over before one o'clock, while you and Steve get some lunch. Step up, Pete, and sit down.'

When the two men had taken their departure, Judge Dewar rocked to and fro in his swivel chair till it creaked in protest. He leaned back with his eyes closed, the cigar clamped in the corner of his mouth trailing a white ribbon of smoke.

Pete tried to relax as he eyed the judge with covert glances during the long silence that seemed eternity. He took a quick look at the clock which read thirty minutes past twelve. Then the chair creaked forward and the long ash fell from the cigar, spilling down the black robe. There was a twinkle in Judge Dewar's eyes as he brushed at the white ash.

'Steve Costello and I were room-mates at law school,' Judge Dewar told Pete. 'You can't room with a man for four years without knowing what's inside him. Steve Costello is a man of honour. You have seen proof of it today. He could have called for a postponement, put Tracy Dunbar on the witness stand and flayed her until she had no shred of pride and honour left. Steve Costello has a chivalry that is outmoded.' He smiled into Pete's eyes. 'Steve tells me he has discovered that rare quality in you. I take his word for it. Your eyes back up his statement.' He dropped the half-smoked cigar into a large brass cuspidor.

'We'll get down to facts, Pete. I'm forced by law to punish you if you are guilty of the crime you are charged with. Tell me, did you shoot and kill Deputy Sheriff Jim West?'

'Yes, sir,' Pete said quietly, his lips quivering. 'I killed him. I'm willing to take my punishment for it.'

'I will have to send you to the Montana State Reformatory in the Deer Lodge Valley until you become of legal age. That will be approximately three years. The punishment for your crime ranges from a minimum of five years to a maximum of twenty-five years in prison. I am reducing it to the five-year minimum, and if your behaviour warrants it, you will be eligible for parole on your legal twenty-first birthday. That's the best I can do for you, Pete.'

'Thank you, sir.' Pete got to his feet. 'I'll do my best to make a hand there. I'm grateful for what you and Mr. Costello have done for me. I'll not let you down. I promise it.' Pete's voice was dry, husky as he stepped down, carrying the chair back with him.

He was all set and ready when Judge Dewar told him to stand. He looked the judge in the eye without flinching while he pronounced sentence in the hushed courtroom. A pregnant silence followed the faint echo of his last words.

Sheriff Ike Niber and Steve Costello took Pete back to his jail cell.

Pete Craven didn't know, of course, that Steve Costello and Judge Dewar had agreed that he'd be better off in reform school than to be set free and at the mercy of Booger Red.

CHAPTER FOUR

Alone in the cell, Pete Craven took off his coat and draped it carefully on the back of the chair. He was removing his tie when he heard the rattle of dishes on a tray down the corridor, and a girl's shrill scream. 'Don't poke your big finger into that cake, Sheriff Ike.' The scream ended in a rippling laugh. 'Don't tease, holding me up while the fried chicken gets cold.'

'Trot along, honey,' the sheriff chuckled. 'I'll get the door unlocked.'

The light in the corridor was grey and dismal. Pete stood beside his bunk as the sheriff opened the door to let the girl in with the laden tray covered with a large white cloth. As she put the tray on the small table the cell door clanged shut and Ike Niber's long legs carried him down the corridor and out of sight, while Pete and the girl stared at one another in embarrassed silence.

She was about sixteen, with thick chestnut brown curly hair and warm brown eyes, almost the exact colour of her hair. There was a sprinkling of freckles across her short nose and flushed tanned cheeks. She had on a spick-and-span brand new white uniform with short sleeves and rubber-soled white tennis shoes. An uncertain smile moved her lips and her voice had an almost frightened tone. 'You don't remember me, do you, Pete?' she said.

'No.' Pete shifted his weight uneasily.

'I'm Nora Moran. Mitch Moran's kid. We went to school together at Catfish Crossing. I was ten when we moved away from our ranch on CK creek, when Zee Dunbar sent my daddy to the pen. Mom owns the CK restaurant here. Sheriff Ike Niber and Judge Dewar set her up in business. Mom does the cooking and I wait on table. That Sheriff Ike is an awful tease, always playing jokes, like locking me in with you now.'

'I remember you, Nora,' Pete told her. 'You used to ride a paint pony to school.'

Nora nodded. 'I sent you a mushy valentine.' She laughed. 'You never spoke to me after that.'

'I was kinda bashful.' Pete grinned, his face reddening.

'Always had your nose in a book.' Nora looked across the table at him. 'You've changed a lot, Pete. You were a skinny kid, the last time I saw you. You're almost a man.'

'I'll be a man, I reckon, by the time I get out of reform school,' Pete said.

'You don't have to go to reform school,' Nora whispered. 'Mom sent me to tell you that Booger Red was in town last night. He came to the kitchen door at the CK and told Mom that he and some more men would get you out of jail before train time. That's around midnight. He said for you to sit tight and be ready when they come. Booger Red said he could trust Mom because she was Mitch Moran's wife and he and Mitch had always been pardners.'

Pete's hand went up to the healed-over quirt welt along his cheek. When he spoke his voice was a harsh croaking whisper.

'I'd rather spend the rest of my life in jail than travel the outlaw trail with Booger Red.' His eyes were narrowed and cold as he looked at the girl. 'Sheriff Ike Niber and the night jailor had better be warned to be on guard. Booger Red's dangerous. I know the tough renegades he travels with—two-bit outlaws like...'

'Like Mitch Moran,' Nora said.

'Booger Red and Mitch Moran. Your dad and my old man. Two-bit horse thieves and cattle rustlers, Nora.'

'Booger Red used to quirt you, Pete,' Nora said. 'My dad never laid a hand on me. He was always bringing Mom and me presents and laughing and teasing us. We never saw him drunk or mean. He's a trustee at the prison farm. He comes up before the Parole Board next month. Judge Dewar told us he'd be turned free.'

Nora Moran's small hands clenched and tears welled in her eyes. Her voice was muffled and choked when she spoke. 'You don't know what we've been through... Mom a convict's widow ... me a jailbird's brat...' The sobbing died out and Nora lifted her head slowly.

Peter Craven got up and took the girl in his arms and kissed her. The quivering lips clung to his, the sob still there, as her arms went up around his neck. Standing like that for a long time, neither of them quite knew or understood what was happening to them. There was no time to reason out the hurt and loneliness, the isolation with all its bitterness, that had built up a protective shell of wariness and suspicion around each of them. Now that crust seemed to have broken and fallen away as they found love and understanding satisfied in each other.

Whatever young Pete Craven had felt in the nearness of Tracy Dunbar had been another thing, altogether different in its chemistry. Pete had in his own way sensed something of Tracy's sophisticated woman tactics: the nearness of her as she taught him to dance, the seductive husky tone of her voice, were as heady as the perfume she used.

With Nora Moran it was something that had suddenly become lasting and mature. Something they both knew and understood without the bother of words, wholly content in their new love. They were standing like that when Steve Costello's voice broke them apart.

'Get back to the CK as quickly as possible, Nora,' the attorney told her. 'Leave the supper tray. Have no worry concerning Pete. Steve Costello always takes excellent care of his clients.'

When Nora had gone he told Pete to put on his hat and coat. 'Wrap the cold chicken in the napkin to eat along the road. You and I are travelling by buggy to Fort Belknap and catching the train for Deer Lodge there. It's seventeen miles by wagon road. We'll have just enough time to make it in three hours. The sooner we start the less risk we run of Booger Red stopping us.'

Pete told the attorney what Nora Moran had told him about the message from Booger Red. Steve Costello already knew about the planned jail break and told Pete that was why they were taking him out now.

Pete saw nobody inside the dimly lit jail as they went outside. They walked a distance, keeping to the dark streets and alleyways until they saw the buggy with a canvas top and side curtains. Porky Jones, the jailor, sat heavily on the seat, a sawed-off shotgun across his lap. Porky belched and yawned as he moved over, handing the lines to Pete.

'You drive, kid,' he said, then motioned towards the attorney. 'Sheriff Ike says for you to go back to town, Steve. Keep your ear to the ground around the saloons while I take the kid to the train. Ike and a few of the boys are layin' low to cut down Booger Red when he shows.'

'So long, Pete.' Steve Costello gripped his hand. 'I'll pay you a visit before long.'

'Thanks for all you've done for me, sir,' Pete said.

'Take care of that boy, Porky,' Steve Costello told the jailor. 'He's worth saving.'

'That all in how a man wants to look at it,' the paunchy jailor growled, belching heavily as the rig drove into the night. 'If Booger Red and his tough renegades block the road, I'll dump you out, kid, and drive on. I don't want no trouble with that old man of yours.'

Pete drove the team of livery stable horses, saying nothing as he edged away from the man whose bulk filled most of the seat, away from his belching stale beer and fried onion breath.

Having declared himself, the fat jailor proceeded to make himself comfortable, the gun across his lap weighted down by the heavy paunch. It wasn't long before he snored, his body limp.

Pete watched ahead as the wagon road followed the banks of Milk River. The cottonwoods were shedding their dry leaves, the leafless branches showing like gaunt old arms with long skeleton fingers pointing into the moonlit sky. Pete tried to find warmth and hope as he conjured up the picture of little Nora Moran.

Porky Jones came awake as the lights of Fort Belknap showed. He lit a match, holding it to his watch. 'We made 'er,' he said. 'And a good half hour to spare. I'll send the livery rig back and ride the train to Chinook with you. The sheriff will take you from there to Deer Lodge.'

CHAPTER FIVE

Pete Craven had never ridden a train. Porky Jones shoved him up the steps, his shotgun cradled in his arm. The Negro porter's eyes bugged out as he picked up his stool and followed them as the train jerked forward.

Porky led the way into the washroom, his gun parting the heavy green curtains as his head nodded his prisoner to follow. Pete blinked his eyes to focus to the lamplight. The jailor's big bulk hid Pete's view of the man who sat at the far end of the upholstered seat along the wall.

'Point that damn scattergun in some other direction,' the man growled.

Pete froze in his tracks as he recognized the voice of Zee Dunbar.

Porky placed the shotgun on the metal wash bowls. As Pete fell sideways from the jolting of the train, he stood face to face with Zee Dunbar.

Zee looked ill at ease in a new suit and starched white collar and necktie. A new Stetson hat was already pulled out of shape. His eyes looked bloodshot as they glared at Pete from under the slanted hatbrim. Zee sat the cushioned seat as he sat his saddle, both feet planted wide apart, leaning a little forward. He gripped the neck of a half empty bottle in one hand, an empty water glass in the other. The butt of a gun in a shoulder holster showed under his coat.

'Sit down, kid,' Porky wheezed. 'Till the porter gets your bed made up. Then you crawl in on the top deck and button the curtains, and stay there till the train leaves Chinook.'

'How come you two got on at Fort Belknap?' Zee said acidly. 'What goes on here, anyhow, Porky?'

'Booger Red was aimin' to break into the

jail and get his kid. Now that his son has killed a man with a law badge, the big tough renegade decides the kid'll do to take along. So we're slippin' Pete off to reform school.'

'Hell, if the kid wants to travel Booger Red's route, let him go.' Zee eyed Pete narrowly.

'It turns out, Zee, that Pete don't want to travel with his old man. He wants no damn part of the outlaw trail.'

Zee Dunbar splashed whisky into the tumbler until it was half filled, his eyes hard as he stared at the glass and swished the liquor around, then lifted it and drank with a methodical slowness. When the glass was drained he filled it again.

'Any chance,' Zee said, without bothering to look up, 'that Booger Red might take a look through the cars when the train stops at Chinook?'

Porky belched. 'There's some risk. That's why I'm hidin' the kid in an upper berth before we pull into Chinook.'

'Lock the kid in my stateroom. If Booger Red boards the train I'll take his mind off his troubles.' Zee looked up as the porter shoved his head through the curtains. 'Show these gents how to get to my stateroom, Arthur.'

'Yassuh, Mister Zee.'

The train whistled and slowed for the next

stop, the cowtown of Chinook. The clang of the engine bell sounded faintly inside the Pullman coach. Porky Jones and Pete followed the Negro porter to the stateroom.

'It's been a long time since Zee Dunbar's been on one of his drunks,' Porky Jones said. 'Where's he headed for, porter?'

'He got a ticket to Butte. Miz Dunbar done went to Butte last night.' The porter backed away and went down the corridor as the air brakes hissed and the train slowed to a halt.

'Lock the door on the inside, kid,' Porky grunted as he pulled it shut, his huge bulk filling the narrow passageway as he moved along, the sawed-off shotgun cradled in his arm.

Pete slipped the catch that locked the door and sat gingerly on the plush cushions, tense as a coiled rattler. He strained his ears against the window when he heard Sheriff Ike Niber's voice outside on the platform.

'... so the damn thing kinda fizzled out like a damp fire cracker. Booger Red can smell a gun trap a mile off. Stayed back in the shadow outa gun range. Sent a couple of half-drunk gunslingers in to do the job. One of my deputies inside the jail got quick triggered, opened up too soon. They made a running fight of it and got clean away.'

'Zee Dunbar's on the train. He let the kid

have the use of his stateroom,' Porky told the sheriff.

'That's mighty generous.' Ike Niber's voice was heavy with bitter sarcasm.

'That ain't the half of it, Ike. Zee's trackin' down his young wife. That range dude gunslinger, Lance Rader, took the same train Zee's missus was on.'

'The hell!' the sheriff said explosively.

'Zee's on the bottle, Ike. He's gunnin' for Rader and he's got a rawhide quirt in his satchel. Looks like Zee's goin' to break his young wife from jumpin' the pasture fence for greener grass. You know what ol' Zee's like when he's drunk, Ike.'

'I got a mind to take him off the train and lock him up and lose the key,' Ike said, his voice whetted sharp.

'It's too late now, Ike. Zee's done got 'er made. Nothin' this side of hell goin' to stop him from killin' that range dude and rippin' the hide off his wife's back. It's been building up for a long time. He'd kill you or any man that got in his way.'

'I'm sending Steve Costello with the kid to Deer Lodge,' said the sheriff. 'You better come with me and we'll see if we can pick up Booger Red's trail.'

The shrill blast of the locomotive whistle drowned out all other sounds. The bell clanged and the train jolted into motion. Pete raised the window blind and looked out. He saw the sheriff and the jailor standing on the plank platform. Sheriff Ike Niber caught sight of Pete through the lamplit window and lifted his arm in a farewell salutation. Porky waved his big hand. Pete forced a grin and waved back. The train picked up momentum and the cowtown of Chinook was left behind in the night.

It was a while before he became aware of the pounding on the locked door. The voice of Steve Costello sounded in the passageway. Pete slid the catch and opened the door. Beyond the tall framed attorney was the frightened face of the Negro porter.

'It's all right, Arthur.' The attorney had Porky's sawed-off shotgun under his arm, a wicker lunch basket in his hand. He put the gun and basket down and reached into his pocket and pulled out a crumpled bank-note.

'No, suh, Cap'n Steve.' The grey-headed Negro shook his head. 'It's a mighty honour and pleasure to have you aboard. Anything you want in the dining-cah, I'll fetch it.'

'There's nothing I can think of at the moment. How's your wife and youngsters, Arthur?' Steve Costello asked.

'Fine, Cap'n Steve,' the white teeth showed. 'They's six of 'em now. There ain't no night yo' name ain't spoke into my wife's prayers.' He moved the palm of his hand across the blue ridge of a knife scar along his jaw. The grin was gone and the dark eyes misted a little. 'There ain't a day passes that I don't remember that you saved me from hangin' in that Butte co't room; the thousand dollars you put in the bank to keep my wife and kids. I ain't teched a drop in eighteen years. I'm a deacon now. Own my own home.' The grin came back as the grey-haired porter closed the door softly.

'A deacon,' Steve Costello smiled softly. 'That's a far cry from the man I defended. Arthur Jackson was close to the top as a middleweight prize-fighter, till he tried to lick John Barleycorn. Booze got the decision. He killed a big Negro with his fists in the ring, over some woman.' Steve Costello laid the shotgun up in the baggage rack. 'Deacon Arthur Jackson has come a long way.' He set the wicker basket on the seat opposite Pete and took a sealed envelope from the inside pocket of his coat. 'Nora Moran said to give you this. Her mother sent the lunch basket.'

Pete remembered the fried chicken in the napkin that bulged his coat pocket. 'I forgot about eating,' he said.

'I'll have Arthur bring you coffee when he makes up your berth in here.'

'It's Zee Dunbar's stateroom,' Pete said. 'Zee said for you to use it. He's got something on his mind that won't let him sleep. Says he wants to hire me as his attorney. He was writing out a cheque for a retaining fee when I left. I caught a glimpse of the round amount of five thousand. Make yourself at home, Pete.' His hand trembled a little as he turned the brass doorknob and let himself out. 'Latch the door. Don't let anyone in but Arthur and myself.'

Pete took Nora's six-page letter from the envelope. His face was a little flushed and there were lights in his grey eyes as he read and re-read every word. When the porter's knock sounded Pete shoved the letter into the inside pocket of his coat and opened the door.

'Cap'n Steve done told me all about it,' Arthur said as he fastened a table between the seats and laid out the lunch from the basket beside the jug of steaming hot coffee he had made in the dining-car galley. 'I got reasons to know what's disturbin' yo' mind and way inside you, boy.' He held his two hands out, slowly clenching them into scarred broken knuckled fists. 'I got these two reasons to jog my memory. Now you eat them vittles while I keep an eye on 'at Mistuh Zee Dunbar. Effin he was to go at Cap'n Steve like he was fixin' to mess him up...' The big Negro left the sentence hang as he slowly relaxed his tightly clenched fists, and left the stateroom, saying he'd be back directly.

Later when Arthur returned he propped open the door, his head cocked a little sideways to listen for any ruckus that might come from the men's washroom, while he talked to Pete in a soft voice.

Arthur Jackson told briefly of his ring battles, spicing the story with humorous anecdotes of fight managers and promoters and the big-time gamblers who won and lost fabulous sums on prize-fights. He sketched in the temptations and pitfalls that awaited a prize-fighter as he gained reputation in the prize-ring. Fabulous tales by a Negro prize-fighter who had fought all comers to reach the champions. His stories concerned a new world, bright with the lights of big cities, darkly shadowed with the alleys and poverty and crime. He had a story-teller's faculty for bringing out the sordidness that ended in the decline of a champion. The killing of a man climaxed the degradation in all its utter stark hopelessness. A Negro who had plumbed the depths.

He had cut both wrists in his cell in the Butte jail one night. He was bleeding to death when Steve Costello, the then great criminal lawyer, came in. He looked upon Steve

Costello as a saviour.

Pete Craven listened on a full belly, the strong coffee keeping him wide awake, forgetting his own troubles.

After he had gone Pete undressed and crawled into bed. All self-pity and bitterness had gone out of him as he looked out the window into the night. Pete Craven knew then that the coming years would pass and be forgotten in the healing process of time.

As long as he kept faith in himself and in men like Judge Dewar and Steve Costello and the Deacon Arthur Jackson, whose deep-toned, soft-voiced story had touched him, Pete Craven had no fear of tomorrow, with the love of Nora Moran there to sweeten his dreams through the coming years.

CHAPTER SIX

Pete Craven came awake, roused from deep slumber by the rapping on the stateroom door and the first call for breakfast in the dining-car.

Before the ranch-raised kid could decide whether or not an answer was expected, the speaker had moved on. Pete got out of bed and as he stuck his head out the door he saw

Steve Costello come out of the men's washroom, the green drapes swinging behind him.

The attorney's lean-jawed handsome ravaged face was clean shaven, his hair freshly trimmed, his suit freshly sponged and pressed. He managed a sort of courtly swagger as he saluted Pete with a wave of his hand. It was only when he brushed past Pete and closed the stateroom door that Pete caught the strong odour of whisky and saw the bloodshot eyes.

'Arthur,' the lawyer rubbed his hand along his cheek, 'gave me the works. He's got Zee Dunbar leaning back in a chair now smothered in hot towels. The poker game broke up at daybreak when a shoe drummer and a liquor salesman got off at Fort Benton, both sadder and wiser men.' Steve pulled crumpled bank-notes from his pockets, tossing them on the unmade berth.

'Wash up, Pete, while I count the net proceeds that, added to Zee's five thousand retainer fee, will put Stephen Costello on a solvent basis. Have you ever been to Great Falls, Pete?' he asked.

'No, sir.'

'Then you have a rare treat in store. We'll lay over in Great Falls till tomorrow.' Steve Costello's eyes were bright with excitement.

He left a neat stack of bank-notes on the blanket, saying, 'Your spending money, Pete.'

Pete saw his new suit where it hung, sponged and pressed on a hanger. The porter had slipped in and out again without waking him.

Breakfast in the dining-car was a wondrous thing for the boy. The Negro waiter never batted an eye when Steve Costello ordered ice-cream for Pete after he'd eaten the omelet and stack of hotcakes drowned in real maple syrup.

Steve Costello had timed it nicely. They had just finished breakfast when the train pulled into the station. There was no sign of Zee Dunbar as they left the train. Pete held out his hand to the porter and felt the firm grip of Arthur Jackson's big hand.

'Take good care of Cap'n Steve, boy,' the soft voice said, ''at man sho' totes a heavy cross. He he'ps others but won't let nobody he'p him tote his heavy burden.' Arthur Jackson tossed his stool up the steps and swung aboard as the train jerked into motion.

A white-haired handsome man had shaken hands with Steve Costello as he stepped off, holding him in conversation until the train pulled out. Steve laid a hand on Pete's shoulders.

'I want you to shake hands, Pete, with United States Senator Paris Gibson, the father of Great Falls. This is Peter Craven, Senator, a sort of protégé of mine. Born and raised on a cow ranch. I'm showing him your city for the first time.'

'You couldn't want for a better guide, Pete,' Senator Paris Gibson gripped the boy's hand, 'nor a truer friend.' Then to Steve Costello he said, 'I want you to give what I've just told you careful consideration, Steve, regarding your becoming Judge of the Supreme Court for Montana.'

'I am deeply honoured, Senator,' Steve Costello said, 'for the high esteem you have of a man who has sold his birthright for a mess of pottage.'

'Nonsense, Steve,' Senator Gibson snorted. 'You are too fine and courageous a man to be weakened by self-pity. I'll meet you later at the Park Hotel.' He gripped the attorney's shoulder.

Steve Costello picked up his shabby gladstone bag from the platform when the Senator had gone. 'They broke the mould,' he said, 'when Paris Gibson was made. A kindly man is rare, hard to find.'

Pete was acutely aware of one outstanding fact that stood out from the rest of the brief exchange of words. Steve Costello had not by word or gesture let on that Pete Craven was a convicted prisoner bound for reform school. But he could not find the right words to express his gratitude for the omission.

That long day was something to remember always. If Pete lived to be old as Methuselah he would never forget any detail of that memorable holiday. The immortal Charlie Russell, with his boots and Red River multi-coloured sash around his waist, hat thumbed back, had drawn a crayon sketch on a big pad as he squatted on the floor of his cabin studio and told stories. It was a likeness of young Pete Craven as he sat a horse. He had torn the canyon picture carelessly from his sketch pad and tossed it to Pete. Pete had stared at it wide-eyed, wondering how the greatest of all Western artists had ever guessed the manner in which he sat a saddle, or knew the dark roan colour of his horse. Even the saddle itself was a detailed replica of his own. When he looked up he found a grin on the artist's face.

'I heard some cowpunchers swappin' yarns in the bunkhouse at the Circle C Ranch in the Little Rockies one day,' he said. 'No need to mention names but they told how a kid named Pete rode a green roan bronc down a trail one night in the lead of a bunch of horses. They described the way you sat the new saddle one of the outlaws had given you. It hung up somewhere in my memory book. Take the sketch back to the ranch when you go.' He spilled Bull Durham flakes into a white rice paper and rolled a cigarette, grinning through the smoke.

'I'm not going back to the ranch. I'm headed for reform school,' Pete blurted out.

'I read about it in the newspaper,' Charlie Russell said, dismissing it in those words as he drew on his sketch pad. 'You'll do your time and go back to the ranch. Maybe I'll come down on your range sometime and have you show me the country. I want to sketch that cabin at the Hideaway.' He ripped the sketch off and tossed it to Pete. It was a rider on a sun-fishing bronc.

'Something to show the kids where you're going, Pete,' he said.

Pete was worn out with all the excitement when he went to bed in the hotel room around midnight. He'd wound up the day by going to a moving picture called *The Great Train Holdup* at the Bijou Theatre.

He was sunk in dreamless sleep in the dark hour before dawn when Steve Costello came in. Undressing in the dark, the lawyer crept into the other big bed and dropped into a restless troubled whisky-fumed sleep.

Pete wakened, the stupor of heavy sleep lingering in the grey light of dawn that came through the open window. He lay there motionless, hearing the muffled sound of Steve Costello's voice in the pillow ... 'Tracy ... Tracy ...'

Then, as if awakened by the sound of his own voice, Steve Costello's head moved and he turned over. He lay there, his head buried in his folded arms and Pete saw the man's hands clench into knotted fists as a dry, choked sound shook the giant body.

Pete lay back quietly, feigning sleep for a long time, turning his face and eyes away from the other bed; knowing that it was something far and away and beyond the whisky that had dragged the once great criminal attorney down from his proud pedestal.

When at long last the attorney threw back the bed covers and moved across the room to the quart bottle on the dresser, Pete sat up and swung his legs over the edge of the bed.

'Just cuttin' the phlegm, Pete,' the lawyer said, coughing and clearing his throat. 'Wake up and listen to the mocking birds. Our train leaves at seven-thirty. I just remembered I left the sawed-off shotgun in Zee Dunbar's stateroom. I hope Zee don't shoot up the train. He's hell on wheels once he gets started. I'll earn that retaining fee if Zee Dunbar gets into trouble.'

CHAPTER SEVEN

The sun was setting when Pete Craven and Steve Costello went through the big gate of the high barbed-wire fence surrounding the cluster of brick buildings of the Montana State Reform School in the Deer Lodge Valley.

The big yard was empty. A guard accompanied them to the building that housed the Superintendent's office. Steve Costello held the door open and Pete Craven walked into the office ahead of him, his heart pounding against his ribs.

The grey-haired man in the swivel chair behind the desk had a slow grin on his face as he got up and held out his hand. It was Old Brocky, the schoolteacher from Catfish Crossing on the Missouri River. There was a glint of genuine pleasure in his puckered eyes as he gripped Pete's hand, and said, 'Sit down, boy. I had a wire saying you were on your way.'

Old Brocky shook hands with Steve Costello. 'It's a pleasure, Steve, to shake your hand again. An honour to have you come here. Pull up a chair and we'll sign Pete in.'

Old Brocky cut Pete a look while he spoke to the lawyer. 'There's some tough kids here.

Pete's coming in under a hell of a handicap. They're all set and ready to size up Booger Red's kid because he killed a man, a law officer at that. They're looking for a leader who'll kick the lid off.' His puckered eyes kept looking at Pete.

'They'll have to find another leader,' Pete said, meeting Old Brocky's sharp scrutiny.

'I'm glad to have your word on that, Pete,' Old Brocky said. 'I hated to hear you got into trouble. On the other hand I was glad you were coming here, right when I need somebody I can trust. You'll have a lot of responsibility saddled on your young shoulders, Pete.'

The icy lump inside Pete was melting now. But there was one thing he wanted cleared up right here and now.

'I don't want any kind of favours, sir,' Pete said. 'It has to be like that.'

'You'll get no favour or privilege you don't earn, Pete. I hold down this job I have here because I've been through the mill. Raised in an orphanage; had to do time in the big house to learn my lesson. I rode with the Hole-in-the-Wall gang; got shot from my saddle while I was holding the horses for three men inside a bank. They rode off and left me in a puddle of blood. Steve Costello defended me; kept me from hanging; then got me paroled.' Old

Brocky's smile was twisted.

Pete kept staring at the two older, grey-haired men in puzzled wonderment. All this was news to him. The look in their eyes as they smiled at one another, sharing a secret that warmed them inside. It tightened Pete's throat a little and his eyes felt itchy like hot sand had blown into them, as the Negro's words came back: 'Cap'n Steve he'ps others ... won't let nobody he'p him tote his heavy burden...'

After Steve Costello had taken his departure Old Brocky took Pete into the big mess hall where the young inmates sat at three long tables eating supper. All wore the same uniform—blue cotton shirts and blue denim Levi overalls and heavy work shoes; the shirts and Levis clean and faded from laundering, the shoes scuffed and worn but brushed clean. All of them had the same short haircut, all with scrubbed faces and hands; all with the same brand of Unwanted. It showed in their eyes and in the sly, furtive or sullen expressions on their faces.

At the head of each table sat a man dressed in a blue uniform like the guard at the locked iron entrance gate.

The clatter of knives and forks and spoons and heavy white chinaware dishes stopped abruptly as every eye in the big room centred and focused on Pete Craven during the long pause before Old Brocky broke the pregnant silence.

'This is Pete Craven,' Old Brocky said. 'You boys give Pete a square deal. Show him the ropes till he gets the hang of the place.'

Pete was uncomfortably aware of himself now. The white soft-collared shirt and the polka dot tie, the double-breasted blue serge suit and his polished black boots. He was a dressed up dude and he read the sneering contempt in the scrubbed face and pale muddy eyes of the big tow-headed kid at the first table. He saw it reflected in the looks of the other kids; an unwelcome mixture of resentment and ridicule and awe and morbid curiosity.

'I know you boys can deal Pete plenty misery,' Old Brocky was saying. 'You make it unshirted hell for a new kid...'

Pete jerked his head back quickly as a tiny pellet struck his cheekbone below his eye. The tiny birdshot carried the sting of a wasp as the tow-headed kid's tongue catapulted it from the gap in his front teeth. Even as Pete felt its sting the lips closed over the discoloured teeth in a faint contemptuous warning sneer. An almost inaudible whispering snicker swept the three tables of youngsters. Pete's hands clenched into fists inside his pants pockets as he eyed the big kid. The fear that had gripped him was gone now and a cold anger had taken its place.

Old Brocky had not taken notice of that almost split-second birdshot incident, or if he had seen, he gave no sign. But his eyes flicked the big tow-head when he said, 'If it comes to a showdown, Pete can take his own part if he's crowded into it.' His hands made a quick gesture. 'That's all. Go back to your grub pile.'

He held the door open and Pete turned his back on the room and walked out. Old Brocky closed the door and took Pete to a big locker room with half a dozen open shower stalls. The place smelled strongly of disinfectant and soap.

A big man with the build of a wrestler came through a door at the far end of the room. He wore a sleeveless shirt and a pair of washed khaki pants belted by a wide harness strap, blackened with old sweat. He wore a pair of old rubber-soled canvas sneakers. He had a splayed nose and a cauliflower ear and his grey clipped hair stood up on his head like hog bristles. A pair of colourless eyes showed from under scar-tissued brows. His wide grin displayed a lot of gold teeth. There was a layer of hard fat over his paunch.

'This is Pete Craven, the new boy I was

telling you about,' Old Brocky said. 'Shake hands with Mike, Pete. Mike used to be a bouncer in a honkeytonk at Havre. Mike's rassled 'em all from Strangler Lewis to Bull Montana. He's head of the guards here; athletic instructor.'

Pete's hand was crushed in the big wrestler's grip. 'Hokay, Pete. Strip,' he said, taking a big rough towel and a small scrubbing brush and soap from a shelf.

Pete took what money he had left from the bank-notes Steve Costello had given him and laid it on a wooden bench, together with a jack-knife, a handkerchief and toothbrush. His face stiffened as he took Nora's letter rolled up in Charlie Russell's sketches from his inside coat pocket.

Old Brocky took a large brown envelope from the side pocket of his coat. 'Put everything in here, Pete. Seal the flap and write your name across it. Nobody'll touch it till you claim it when you leave.'

Pete undressed quickly and stood under the hot shower as he lathered himself from head to foot and scrubbed. He took the cold needle shower until the goose flesh showed, then towelled till the glow of warmth came back. He dressed in the wool underwear and blue shirt and denim overalls, the white cotton socks and heavy cowhide shoes the reform school furnished. Mike gave him a folded white nightshirt.

The barracks was a wooden barn-like structure, with rows of double bunks along two sides. The beds were made up in army fashion. The upper bunk was for clothes and books and magazines. A dim light shed a faint glow into the room, leaving dark shadows. There were no bars across the open windows. Every boy was in his bunk and the buzzing hum of whispering stopped as Mike showed Pete to his bunk.

Pete undressed quickly and pulled on his nightshirt and crawled in between the blankets. As he pulled the blankets up the bare cold room echoed with a raucous chorus of practised snoring, sounding for all the world like a frog-pond din. Then the dimmed light went out.

Pete lay tensed, wide-eyed on his bunk as he stared into the darkness. It happened without warning in the covering din of the snoring. The mattress was jerked from under him, the blankets ripped off. Pete landed on the board floor with a dull thudding sound. He rolled up on to his hands and knees and was scrambling to his feet as a heavy bulk landed on his back. Pete fell on his face as the weight straddled him. Hands gripped his hair, slamming his face into the bare plank floor.

Pain shot into his head and eyes as his nose bone cracked. He was blinded and dizzy as he was rolled onto a blanket and tossed up in the darkness, high into a black void to the frog-pond chorus of snoring.

'Jiggers!' a harsh whisper sawed through the raucous snoring.

Peter was tossed high again. This time there was no tightly held blanket to break the fall. He landed on the flat of his back on the planks, stunned, his wind knocked out, gasping for breath, the blood from his smashed nose trickling into his mouth. He rolled over to keep out of his own blood as the lights came on. Pete got to his feet as Mike stood there without lending a hand. The pain hammering into his head, Pete flung the mattress back on his bunk and gathered his scattered blankets. He kept his head bent to keep the dripping blood from the bedding. The anger inside him had driven most of the pain away as he crawled into bed without having uttered a sound. He saw Mike turn and walk away, leaving a dim light burning as he went out.

Pete used the tail of his nightshirt to stop the blood that had ebbed to a trickle. His nostrils were clogged and he breathed through his open mouth while the throbbing aching pain racked his bruised body. Under the blankets he worked his legs to make certain there was no broken bones. After that, he lay there moving as little as possible, fighting back the nausea that crept into his mouth that was as dry as dirty clay. Sometimes the exhaustion of pain caused him to doze off, only to come awake shivering as the cold clammy sweat chilled him.

The loud clang of the bell sounded in the first grey light of dawn and Pete heard the kids pile out of their bunks. Every bone and muscle of his body ached as he crawled out and dressed. His whole face felt stiff, his nose swollen across his cheekbones. Both eyes were bloodshot, slitted in discoloured puffs as he followed the others into a big washroom. Nobody spoke to him or took notice of his face except with quick darting furtive glances.

He had washed the blood from his face and hair by the time the second bell clanged and he fell in place at the end of the double line outside the mess hall.

Pete wolfed his grub in grim silence, washing it down with pale chicory from a big mug. The big bowl of oatmeal with a sprinkling of coarse brown sugar and skimmed milk had a soured taste, the stewed prunes were half cooked, the sliced bread dried out. Pete managed to eat most of it before the guard jerked the cord on the fire alarm bell on the outside wall. The kids swung their legs over the long benches and stood at attention, then the blast of a whistle, and they marched out single file.

Pete caught sight of Old Brocky and a short-legged fat man in a wrinkled white jacket as they came from the office building. They started at the head of the line and walked along slowly.

Old Brocky had a paper clamped to a short board, a stub of pencil in his hand. The fat man wore no hat and his bald head with its fringe of drab-coloured hair took on a reddish glow from the early sun. He had a stethoscope in the side pocket of the white jacket that had faded brown iodine spots on it. His bloated red-jowled face had a purplish cast to it and he wheezed with each short-legged step. There was a half-smoked soggy cigar clamped in a corner of his mouth as he waddled along ahead of Old Brocky, eyeing each boy as he passed.

He pulled up short when he came to Pete. He stood close wheezing the sour stench of stale cigar and whisky into Pete's face as his small pouched eyes looked at the battered face. Then the pudgy hand went across the boy's swollen cheeks and without warning the stubby thumbs pressed toward one another on either side of the swollen broken nose.

It felt to Pete like a vice closing with

relentless tortured pressure. The dull click shot pain like white-hot needles into Pete's eyes and head. Blood spurted, spraying the white jacket as Pete fought the dizzy pain, the waves of nausea that broke into cold sweat as he swayed, bracing his legs, and the fat doctor became a blur.

He felt the sting of iodine-soaked cotton swabbing his face. It acted as a counter-irritant to clear the blur from his eyes as the doctor put a pair of thin, flat tongue depressors along either side of his nose, fastening them with strips of adhesive tape. For a fat man the doctor had moved swiftly without a single lost motion.

'Sit down on the steps, kid.' He wiped the blood and iodine from his hand on a wad of gauze, satisfied with a job well done. 'If you feel like pukin' let 'er come. You got guts to spare, kid. One of you kids bring him a dipper of water.' The doctor waddled on down the line chewing on his sodden cigar butt.

Pete shook off the hands of the kid that held him. The fifty-foot distance to the barrack steps seemed a long ways off but he managed to make it. He sat down on the wide step, his head lowered to let the blood from his nose drip on the ground. Gradually the waves of dizziness went away and the nausea churning his stomach settled. He spat out the bitter taste in his mouth and lifted his head.

An undersized freckle-faced kid stood there holding a dipperful of water, an uncertain grin on his snub-nosed face, a sort of pleading look in his red-brown eyes. Then he turned his head quickly to look behind him as if to make certain nobody was within hearing distance.

'Cottoneye Savage,' he whispered as he handed Pete the water, 'is an overgrown yellow-backed bully. He's licked every kid here, from the big ones down to the runt. That's me. Cottoneye's layin' for you, Pete. He fights dirty and he's got a knife buried in the corner of the yard where he'll jump you. Don't let on I told you. He'd skin me alive.'

'I won't squeal on you, kid.'

'Call me Stub. Stub Slade. I'm named for me old man, the jockey. He got killed on the Butte race-track. Maw worked on the line in Butte. Her name Goldie was over the door. I made money runnin' errands for the girls along crib row. Then I got a job as call boy for the railroad. I got caught with a bunch of kids breakin' into a boxcar. The others got away, but they collared me. With my old man dead and Maw workin' on the line, I didn't stand a snowball's chance in hell. I been here two years, since I was fourteen. Goldie took poison and died. If ever I get out I'm going to be a jockey. I got the build and I got the guts.' A grin spread the wide mouth. 'I never been on a horse, Goldie never let me go near the race track,' he admitted. 'You're a cowboy, Pete. Will you learn me how to ride a horse some day?'

Pete rinsed his mouth and spat out the water and drank.

'Sure,' he said. 'Sure thing, Stub.'

'I better get back,' Stub said. 'Remember what I told you about Cottoneye's knife. He can dig it up quick.'

Stub moved off around the corner as a guard came towards Pete.

'The Old Man wants to see you,' the guard told Pete. 'Wash up and Mike will give you a clean shirt.' He walked away, a faint grin on his face.

When Pete walked into the washroom, he saw Cottoneye and four more of the bigger boys with mops and scrub pails. They were barefooted, the legs of their denims rolled up to the knees. The soapy water on the floor was ankle deep and smelled strongly of disinfectant.

Pete halted in the doorway for a brief moment, then went in. They paid no attention until he was at the wash trough rolling up his sleeves, then the mops were laid aside and they formed a half circle as they came towards him. When they were in a tight circle,

Cottoneye came slowly toward Pete, halting just beyond reach.

'Make a fist, Craven.' One muddy eye looked at him, the other milky, filmed and blind in a scarred socket. 'Let's see you make a fist.'

Pete twisted around slowly until his back was against the wide plank wash trough. He braced his legs, the thick soles of his new shoes slippery on the wet cement. He doubled both fists and felt the chill creeping into his belly. As he squared off into a fighting stance he could feel the rapid pounding of his heart under sore ribs.

Pete was puzzled, wary, as the big kid put his hands behind his back. Grinning, he shuffled his bare feet forward in the water and bending over until his face was within inches of Pete's left fist that was cocked and ready to punch, Cottoneye sniffed a couple of times, then stepped back quickly, letting out a short taunting laugh.

'Smells sweet and harmless. Soft as a baby's bottom. Innocent as a virgin's breath.' His chuckle sounded obscene. 'We got a virgin amongst us, boys. Tell us, Craven have you ever ...' Cottoneye stepped back a little, mouthing obscenities, stringing dirty words together in a meaningless string of filth, while the four others grinned and made lewd gestures.

Pete Craven was accustomed to blasphemy and cursing, but this dirty talk was beyond all that he had ever heard. Cottoneye was using words and phrases Pete had never heard and therefore was ignorant of their exact meaning. He stood braced for a sudden rush, eyeing them coldly, a little contemptuously until the game lost its vile flavour.

'I looked up the name Craven in the big dictionary,' Cottoneye changed his tactics. 'It means a coward. Your name ain't Pete here, see. It's Craven. Any kid I hear callin' you Pete or anything but Craven gets bumped till he walks spread-legged for a week.' His big frame bulked as he clenched his fists.

'You spill your guts to the Old Man about what happened last night you'll be sorry. We got a grapevine here that'll tell us if you squeal, Craven.'

Pete felt cold and shaky inside as he stood there eyeing them. 'You're not throwing any scare into me,' he said from behind clenched teeth. 'That ain't the reason I'll keep my mouth shut.' He looked into the muddy eye and its milky mate.

'You think you built up a tough rep by killin' a law man,' Cottoneye sneered. 'My old man was hung for killin' a cop. I'm here because I knifed a man. I'd a ripped his guts out but the cops hauled me off. One of 'em slugged me in the eye with a blackjack. You don't look so tough to me, Craven. Before I go over the hill I'll whittle you down to size. You'll hold your guts in your hand and that's a promise. Wash up and drag your dirty tail over to the Old Man.' Cottoneye picked up his mop, saying, 'Let's get this latrine, jail birds.'

They sloshed and splashed the dirty water all over Pete until he gave up the job of trying to wash. They made way for him, taunting him as he went out.

Mike was in the locker room as he stripped to the hide and stepped into a shower stall. The hot water and the cold needle shower put new courage into him. Mike tossed him a towel as he came out. When he was rubbed dry, Mike beckoned him from a small room.

'Hokay, Pete. Get hon de table. I'll rub de sore knots hout, eh?'

Mike had a complete new outlay of clothing ready, but before Pete pulled on his undershirt, Mike ran a pair of coarse hair clippers across his head, explaining as he worked that he was official barber.

The boys were in classrooms when Pete Craven walked across the yard to the building of the Superintendent. The guard who had told him he was wanted was standing just inside the office with his back to the open door. A lean, wiry-built man with a pockmarked face and a pair of eyes that kept shifting away and coming back to meet those of Old Brocky, who was saying, 'Nobody's accusing you of anything, Nelson. But somebody's passing on to the boys here things that go on inside my office, confidential things.' Old Brocky's eyes were penetrating.

'I quit this job five years ago because I was unable to get the co-operation and financial aid from the Board of Directors. A month ago a new Board of Directors hired me back at an increased salary and I have their permission to discharge any and all employees here.' His fist banged down on his desk. 'Pass that information on, Nelson. That's all. Go back to your job.'

Pete got a good look at Nelson's pockmarked face as he stepped aside to let him pass. There was a white rim around the lipless mouth, an ugly look in his eyes that flicked a glance at Pete as he walked away cracking his big knuckled hands.

Old Brocky's eyes still glinted with cold anger as Pete came in and closed the door. 'That mess of swill you sat down to at breakfast,' he said, 'wasn't fit for a stray dog to eat. The man in charge of the mess hall has been knocking down plenty on the buying of food. There's always a chance for graft in an institution like this.' Old Brocky was voicing his thoughts aloud as he stuck a sheaf of bills on a long spike attached to a heavy lead base.

'Somebody knows the combination to that safe,' he said. 'It was opened last night and on other nights.' His voice sounded gritty. He looked up at Pete with a grim smile.

'They sure gave you the works, Pete. You want to tell me what happened?'

'No, sir,' Pete answered quietly.

'That Cottoneye Savage is the pack leader and jealous of any kid that's big and tough enough to lick him. He don't lose any time putting a new kid in his place. You'll either take him to a cleaning or take his bullying. I reckon you know that, Pete.'

'Yes, sir.'

Old Brocky opened a desk drawer and took out a large hard rubber nose guard with an elastic band.

'Doc Cole said to give you this. Keep it somewhere out of sight, until Cottoneye tackles you for a scrap before that busted nose has a chance to heal. Try it on for fit.'

Pete adjusted the nose guard, clamped his teeth over the hard rubber mouthpiece. Then he removed it and put it inside his shirt.

'Mike says Cottoneye is yellow inside. Go after him, Pete, till you tap it. But that wasn't the reason I sent for you.' Old Brocky unfolded the Deer Lodge Valley newspaper and spread it out on the desk so that the black headlines showed: PROMINENT CATTLEMAN SHOT.

It told about Zee Dunbar, wealthy cattleman, being shot down on the station platform in Butte as he alighted from the train shortly before dawn yesterday morning. His assailant, hidden in the black shadows of the baggage truck, fired from ambush without warning. As the rancher slumped to the platform badly wounded, he managed to draw his gun from its shoulder holster and return the gunfire. Lying in a widening pool of his own blood, Zee Dunbar emptied his six-shooter at the hidden gunman who escaped in the darkness.

Zee Dunbar, questioned by railway detectives and city police, refused to identify the man who shot him by name, but he admitted he knew who it was.

Mrs. Zee Dunbar, who was notified at the Thornton Hotel where she was staying for a week while on a shopping tour in Butte, refused to make a statement of any sort when interviewed by reporters. She and Zee Dunbar's lawyer, Stephen Costello, were at the wounded cattleman's bedside. The latest report from the hospital was that Zee Dunbar lay in a coma in an extremely critical condition, paralysed from the waist down.

The police were combing the city for trace of the gunman, who was thought to be in hiding.

Pete Craven, leaning over to read the newspaper account, straightened up slowly.

'You got any notion who it was shot ol' Zee?' asked Old Brocky.

Pete started to say something; to say it could have been Lance Rader. But he changed his mind. After all it was not for him to name the man.

'If Zee Dunbar kept his mouth shut,' Pete said flatly, 'I reckon it's none of my business.'

CHAPTER EIGHT

Cottoneye made his move one grey day with a raw wind blowing the threat of a snowstorm. It was the exercise hour. The smaller boys were playing leap-frog in a wide circle. Cottoneye and his gang were at the far corner playing basketball, six men to a team. It was Mike's day off and he had gone to town. Nelson had taken his place and he was refereeing the game. Now and then, when a foul was made, the police whistle hanging by a cord around his neck blasted the air.

Pete and a half-dozen other kids were trotting single file around the worn path that followed the fence in order to keep warm. Pete was setting the pace and after a quarter-hour it became a sort of endurance race. One by one they dropped out, winded, their leg muscles tired and aching. Little Stub Slade was the only one left. He trotted behind Pete's long stride. Both had gotten their second wind, sweating a little.

'Last lap, Stub,' Pete called back as they neared the basketball players.

The police whistle blasted to end the game. Cottoneye tossed the ball towards Nelson and as if it had been prearranged, he and the others trotted towards the corner of the fence as Pete and Stub approached.

'Turn back, Stub,' Pete called back in a low tone. 'Run like hell for the barracks. This is it, Jockey.'

Instead of turning back, Stub sprinted ahead and passed the jog-trotting Pete like a streak. He reached the corner of the fence ahead of Cottoneye and his gang.

Pete saw Stub stumble and go down, rolling over and over into the corner of the barbed-wire fence. He started clawing the dirt with both hands with frantic haste for the knife he knew Cottoneye had buried there. When Cottoneye came up at a run and saw what Stub was doing, he slid to a halt, then jumped a few feet off the ground and his heavy soled shoes came down on Stub's small hands.

Pete heard the thin scream as it tore from Stub's mouth. Without halting in his now quickened stride, Pete took the rubber nose guard from inside his shirt and fastened it in place, his teeth clamping on the rubber mouthpiece. Pete lowered his head a little as he put on a last burst of speed and crashed into Cottoneye as he straightened up, the knife in his hand.

They went down together. Pete's cocked fist landed flush on Cottoneye's nose and mouth. It was a vicious savage blow that had all Pete's weight behind it and an added momentum as he fell with the punch. He felt the stab of pain from broken knuckles shooting up into his shoulder. He heard the dull crack of Cottoneye's nose as it broke; saw the blood spurting into the air.

Pete straddled the heaving bulk, riding it as he would a bronc. Using his other hand, he ripped his knuckles into the big buck teeth and Cottoneye's wild screams choked on his own blood as the broken teeth lodged in his throat. His legs kicked and threshed in a desperate frantic effort to free himself of Pete's straddled weight. His big arms flailed and his right hand gripped the knife.

The Dirty Dozen were grouped around in a tight circle. Little Stub Slade sat on the ground beyond, his arms raised to hold up his broken-boned torn hands. There was no fear showing in his eyes as he struggled to his feet to face Nelson who stood there, the loop of a shot-loaded blackjack swinging from his hand.

'Blow the whistle!' Stub shouted.

As Nelson swung the blackjack, Stub ducked away, dodging the reaching arm as he ran around the circle of kids. It was then he saw the burly figure in the white turtle-necked sweater coming through the gate. 'Mike!' Stub shrilled. 'Hurry, Mike!'

When Nelson saw Mike coming on the run he blew the whistle. 'Break it up, you punks!' he yelled. 'Scatter and run, and by God keep your traps shut.'

Pete felt himself jerked and lifted clear. He heard a voice as if it came from a long ways off. 'Hokay, Pete! You de Champ! You don't need to kill Cottoneye! Hokay, Nelson. Pick up your hunk of yellow blubber and take him away.'

The grin on his battered face died as he caught sight of little Stub Slade.

'If you did dat to Goldie's kid, Nelson,' the big fists clenched, 'I'll tear you apart.'

'No, Mike!' Nelson backed away. 'The kid

fell down running a race with Pete. Cottoneye stepped on him by accident.'

Mike picked Stub up in his wrestler's arms, carrying him like a father would carry a baby. 'Hokay, Pete, we take the jockey over to de doc.'

Doctor Cole's hands were swift and deft as he attended to Stub's crushed fingers. Later, when he examined Pete's nose, his fingers were gentle. There was no real damage to the broken nose. New splints were put on and fastened with adhesive tape. He had given little Stub a pill to ease the pain, and told Pete to put him to bed in the barracks.

The doctor's eyes hardened as he looked at the blubbering Cottoneye who sat on the floor, his back against the wall.

'Climb up on the butcher block, Cottoneye,' Doctor Cole wheezed. 'I'll try to live up to the nickname of Drunken Butcher you and your gang have hung on me.'

At the first touch of the doctor's hands on his battered face, Cottoneye let out an agonized howl. 'Don't! Don't! You're tryin' to kill me! Lemme up you drunk sawbones bastard!'

As Pete led Stub across the yard his whisper sounded in the cold black wind, 'They're out to get me, Pete. They'll kill me when it comes.'

Pete put his arm across the boy's shoulders. 'How come they're after you, Jockey?' he asked.

'I was there when Nelson and two other guards and Cottoneye gave a kid the water cure, then locked him up in the black hole. He was dead when they unlocked the door next morning. They left him there until dark, then carried him out and buried him. Nelson stole the kid's record on file in the office and destroyed it. The word passed by grapevine never to mention the kid's name. He was an orphan. He didn't have any parents, anybody to ask questions. When those in charge of the school made enquiry about his disappearance, Nelson and the others had it made. Bobbie Hunt went over the hill, made a clean getaway. Cottoneye and me are the only kids who know Bobbie Hunt was murdered. I'm scared, Pete.'

'Does Mike or Old Brocky know about it, Stub?'

'No. They came here later.'

'The only thing to do, Stub, is to tell Old Brocky what you know.'

'No. I'm no rat. Don't tell what I told you, Pete.'

'I won't tell anybody, Jockey,' Pete promised.

CHAPTER NINE

There was a dangerous tension building up slowly during the following weeks. There was a constant ugly threat in Cottoneye's muddy eye, a dirty film over the blind one. Wherever he went he was tailed by the Dirty Dozen he held together in a bondage of fear and constant veiled threats. The pockmarked Nelson walked warily whenever Mike was within sight or earshot.

Cottoneye, in spite of his ignominious defeat and whipping, was still the leader.

Nobody but Stub Slade had the guts to side openly with Pete Craven. He was Pete's shadow. He now slept in the upper bunk over Pete's bed.

Mike was on duty every night now at the barracks. At irregular intervals his bulky shadow could be seen as he went down the line of bunks, his rubber-soled canvas shoes making no sound.

There was the disquieting rumour that a big break was being planned and whenever it came it would coincide with a big prison break at the Deer Lodge Penitentiary a few miles away in the same valley as the reformatory.

Old Brocky told Pete that Zee Dunbar had

recovered from his bullet wounds and had gone back to his ranch with his wife.

A letter had come for Pete from Nora Moran, telling him that her father had been paroled that morning. Mitch Moran and his wife and Nora were going away to some place where nobody knew them, they'd change their name and get a new start. This would be her last letter. The girl's tears had blurred the inked words that declared her love for Pete Craven but for the safety of her father and mother this had to be the end. For Pete it was a gunshot.

His bitter grief was mixed with an unreasoning hatred for Mitch Moran and every other convict and criminal inside the grey walls of the Deer Lodge prison, or the uncaught outlaws like Booger Red. Mitch Moran had no right to come between Nora and himself. The anger and frustration writhed inside like a poisonous slimy snake. He cursed in silent futile cold fury that left him white-lipped and shaking as he railed against the barriers that outlaws like Mitch Moran and Booger Red had thrown up like a high stockade to hold him here a prisoner.

He cursed and condemned, holding the bitterness and hatred inside him, till he felt sick with a hopeless morbid depression. It added nothing in the way of lightening the burden of bitter grief when he realized in the damning of these criminals he was condemning himself. He had killed a man. He was doing time for his crime. He couldn't lay the blame on Mitch Moran for his being here.

Pete Craven walked the fence like a caged animal, head lowered, eyes staring with brooding thought. Little Stub Slade trotting along behind, watched him with troubled eyes, not knowing the cause of it, not questioning it. All Stub knew was that Pete had received a letter with bad news and he was toughing it out in his own way.

Little Stub's freckled face was pinched and blue from the cold, his eyes watery. His leg muscles were aching and cramped, his cold feet leaden inside the heavy cowhide shoes.

Pete and Stub had the yard to themselves. The other boys, the exercise period ended, had sought the warmth of the barracks room. Stub could see them at tables or on bunks in the first lamplight of approaching dusk. He could see big Mike as he sat back in his armchair reading the pink sheets of the *Police Gazette*.

A stitch in his side shot pain through Stub's belly, slowing him down to a lurching halt in front of the barracks.

'I'm going in, Pete,' Stub called out, gasping a little. 'I got a side ache from trotting.' The wind whipped the words, scattering the sound.

If Pete heard he gave no sign as he went on alone, fighting the turmoil inside him, oblivious of everything in the remote black world that surrounded his isolation.

It was not until the early darkness of approaching night closed in that Pete pulled up in front of the barracks, aware now that he ached in every cramped muscle, that he was cold to the bone, his face stiffened with frostbite.

'Time we went in, Stub,' Pete's voice had a dry-throated croak as he peered around in the darkness. 'Stub!' Pete raised his voice. 'Where are you, Jockey?' A gust of sand and snow-driven wind tore the words to shreds.

Alarmed now, Pete stumbled up the steps and into the storm shed and into the barracks. He pulled up short in the doorway, blinking his eyes against the yellow glare of the big kerosene lamp that hung from the ridge log.

There was a strange hush in the big barn-like room. The smaller boys were grouped together in white-faced, wide-eyed silence. The bigger boys were back up against the far wall, standing with awkward stiffness. Mike's big bulk was bent over Pete's bunk, the leather braces creased into the red flannel-shirted heavy muscled back. As he straightened up, twisting the clipped head on its bull neck, Pete caught a brief glimpse of little Stub Slade on the bunk, the freckles standing out like black warts on the white face with the closed eyes.

'Pete!' Mike's voice was harsh. 'Where you been? Never mind. Fetch Doc!'

Pete turned quickly and sprinted across the yard for the infirmary. Doctor Cole was in his shirt-sleeves, standing at the sink in the emergency room, pouring himself a drink from a quart bottle of bonded whisky.

'Quick, Doc!' Pete said. 'Stub's sick or hurt.'

Doc tossed down his drink and put the bottle in the cupboard. He picked up his worn shabby black bag and followed Pete.

Mike stood aside as the doctor came up. He said, 'De little jock found de fire in de furnace room. He had de hose turned on and de fire put out when dey jumped him and give him de works. Only for Stub de whole damn barracks woulda been afire, and dese kids in here burned alive.' Mike grabbed Pete's arm.

'Hokay, Pete. Let's go. Doc can manage.'

They met Old Brocky in the hall. His face was set in grim lines and his eyes were slivers of blue ice. There was a greyish pallor to his leathery skin. He had a cartridge belt and six-shooter strapped on, a sawed-off double-barreled riot gun in the crook of his arm.

'I jumped six guards in their quarters,' he explained. 'They were waiting for Nelson. They never got a chance to use their knives and blackjacks. They're locked in the furnace-room where Nelson and Cottoneye set the fire. Stub Slade flooded the furnace-room with the hose or the place would have been burned to the ground.'

Mike said, 'Doc's with Stub. De little jock's takin' the last count.' Mike's voice caught in a dry sob.

'I've turned on the big searchlight, Mike,' said Old Brocky. 'I've telephoned the warden at the pen, notified the sheriff in town. The fire at the reform school was to be the signal that touched off the big break at the pen. It was the exercise hour before supper at the prison when all convicts would be in the yard. Stub Slade nipped it in the bud when he put out the fire. Every spare guard at the prison would have been sent over here to fight fire and with night closing in and the cells not yet locked for the night, with guns waiting on the outside, it would have been pickin's for the six tough convicts who planned to break out.'

'They picked a hell of a night,' Mike said. 'By now it's a blizzard outside.'

'They had no choice. The date was set months ago for November 1st, between the hours of four-thirty and five, the exercise period, come hell or blizzard or ten-foot snowdrifts.

'Several paroled convicts were released this morning. They walked out free men. But weeks before they'd made the necessary arrangements for a fast getaway and a safe hideout for a half-dozen of their convict friends in on the big break. They'd passed the word to their wives and sweethearts and friends who came to visit them to have guns and ammunition outside the prison walls. This blizzard was to their advantage. The snow would cover the tracks.'

'You talk like you and de warden was hep, Boss,' said Mike.

'There was a leak,' Old Brocky admitted. 'Every convict paroled this morning was tailed when he went out the prison gate. I put new padlocks on the reform school gate this evening and told the guard to go to his quarters; that there was no need for him to shiver inside the gate-house in this storm. The sheriff sent a couple of mounted deputies to ride patrol outside the fence. That's why there is no need for you to go in search of Nelson and Cottoneye who have turned up missing.'

'I'm goin' out for air, Boss.' Mike put on a big muskrat fur coat and mackinaw and four-buckle overshoes. 'If dat Nelson or Cottoneye are inside de fence, I'll find 'em.'

Old Brocky scowled, knowing there was no way of stopping big Mike. 'Take this,' he said, holding out the riot gun.

'I don't need no gun,' Mike said, raising his big hands. 'I got dese.' He headed for the door.

'I'd like to go along,' Pete spoke up.

'You stay here, son,' Old Brocky said flatly. 'That letter you got this afternoon had a Deer Lodge postmark. I didn't open it before I gave it to you.' He smiled mirthlessly.

'It was from Nora Moran, Mitch's daughter,' Pete said.

'Mitch Moran was one of the paroled convicts. Like the others, he's under suspicion. His wife and daughter registered at the hotel in Deer Lodge last night under a different name. It was only when Mitch trailed there that the law discovered who they were.'

Without hesitating Pete handed the letter to Old Brocky, saying, 'Read it.' He turned away abruptly and went into the barracks.

'Stub wants to talk to you, Pete,' the doctor said, as Pete came in.

Stub's pain-seared eyes lighted up as Pete gripped the hand he held out. A smile tugged his mouth.

'It's my fault, Stub,' Pete said as he sat

down in a chair the doctor shoved behind his knees. 'I didn't know you were gone...'

'It wasn't anybody's fault, Pete. I got a side ache and came in. Mike was asleep and I didn't want to wake him up. When I smelled smoke I went down to the cellar. I saw the blaze behind the smoke coming from the furnace-room door and turned the fire hose into the room. I had a tight hold on the big nozzle to keep it from jerking out of my hand when somebody turned the water off. Then Cottoneye and Nelson grabbed me. Said they were going to kill me to keep me from squealing about how they murdered Bobbie Hunt. It was bad. When Mike smelled the smoke and came on the run, he scared them off before they finished the job. I'm no rat, Pete. And I ain't scared to die.'

'You're not going to die, Stub.' Pete tried to make the words sound convincing. 'When we get out, I'm getting you a horse and teaching you to ride. You'll be the best jockey ever rode a race, Stub. You can't go back on the deal we made.'

'I was stringing you along, Pete,' a smile twisted his mouth. 'Stringing myself along. I kept lying to myself, making believe, trying to fool myself and you, too, Pete. I'm scared of horses. I saw what was left of my old man when they carried his bloody broken body off the track in a horse blanket. I still wake up nights with the cold sweat all over me. I'm scared to even hold a halter rope. I'm yellow inside, Pete.'

'Yellow, hell,' Doctor Cole spoke up. 'That's a hell of a way for a hero to talk. You had the guts to hang on to the bucking twisting nozzle of a fire hose, breathing smoke into your lungs, till you got the fire out. It's that red-hot smoke you breathed that's causing the trouble now. Mike and every kid caught in this fire-trap owes his life to little Stub Slade.' The doctor lowered his voice as he bent over the bunk.

Stub Slade's eyes were on Pete's as the hand of death passed over them, a soft smile on the boy's lips. Doctor Cole pulled the blanket up over his face.

Pete quit his chair and crossed the room, to stand staring out the screen-meshed storm windows into the night. The searchlights from the wall of the distant prison stabbed streaks of slowly moving white light into the black blizzard. The giant horns on the prison roof split the silence with a banshee wailing.

The searchlight on the roof of the superintendent's building at the reform school moved slowly on its rotating axis along the wire fence.

The glare found big Mike in mackinaw and

fur cap as he walked around the fence, head lowered, gorilla arms with clenched fists swinging heavily with each stride. The pockmarked Nelson and Cottoneye Savage had escaped. Cottoneye had kept his promise to go over the hill and he'd taken his tough mentor along.

As the blizzard swept down Deer Lodge Valley and across the town it carried with it the added threat of escaped convicts as the raucous warning of the horns screamed hideous alarm. Window blinds in every house were pulled to blacken out the lamplight within. Doors were locked and barred. Guns were taken from racks and loaded. The long dreaded, secretly whispered big prison break had come.

As Pete stared out the window he thought of those few weeks little Stub Slade had crept into his heart to fill an empty void there. Stub had been the only close friend he had ever known. Now he had gone away forever and he had taken something along with him that Pete had given him as a farewell gift. It was an intangible nameless thing they had shared together in their loneliness, a comradeship given and taken and shared equally.

A poignant bitterness, born of regret and self-accusation, as he recalled that last hour shared together, knifed through him. He was to blame for what had happened to little Stub. He had caused the death of his friend. Nelson and Cottoneye had jumped the little jockey while he was walking the fence feeling sorry for himself. The tortured self-condemnation showed in his eyes that stared out with a stricken unseeing look into the black night.

A strange hush had fallen over the room. Pete caught sight of Mike as he stood outside facing into the wind-whipped snow, letting the force of the blizzard whip his face with its freezing blast. It came to Pete's troubled mind that Mike, too, was blaming himself for falling asleep in his chair and allowing Stub to leave the room to be submitted to the torture that resulted in his death.

Big Mike, who feared nothing on earth, blaming himself as Pete did, was taking his own self-inflicted punishment for his negligence. Mike had known Stub's parents when he was a professional wrestler and bouncer at various honkeytonks. He had given them money whenever they had asked for it, and he had done his best to look after their boy who never had a chance from the time he was born in a bed in a house of prostitution.

Doctor Cole laid a hand on Pete's shoulder. 'Fetch Mike in,' he said, 'before he breathes too much of that blizzard into his lungs.

Those barrel-chested men go fast when pneumonia set in.'

Somehow the doctor's words had lightened some of the leaden burden inside Pete. He tried to pass it on to Mike as he picked up the mackinaw and fur cap Mike had taken off and dropped in the snow to feel the full force of the icy blast. Pete took Mike's arm and led him into the barracks, telling him what the doctor had said.

The mounted deputies had ridden through the gate and fastened it shut. They'd put their horses in the stable and come inside.

'This place is going to get as cold as an ice house if that furnace don't get fired up,' Mike said. 'I'll put the locked-up guards to work.'

Mike told the two deputies to stand at the door of the furnace-room, their guns ready. He swung the door wide and tossed in mops and buckets and hung a lantern over the door to light the room. He ordered two guards to get the furnace lit and keep it going, and told the other four to mop the furnace-room floor.

Old Brocky handed Mike the sawed-off riot gun and motioned Pete to follow him. When he reached a window at the far end of the building that commanded a view of the whole yard, he stood there looking out, his face grim lined, his puckered eyes as bleak as the blizzard outside.

The distant searchlights from the prison walls were no more than dim blobs of light now, but they could hear the giant klaxons blast their warning at two- or three-minute intervals.

Pete Craven stood beside the older man, not daring to break his brooding thoughts. The lonesome sound of a locomotive whistle wailed in the stormy night. Old Brocky took his watch out and consulted it.

'That'll be number seven, the Westbound Limited, pulling out,' he said. 'I hope to God Mitch Moran and his missus and kid are safe aboard.' The grizzled head turned away and he spoke without taking his stare from the window, 'I made mention of a leak in the prison grapevine, Pete. Mitch Moran was the convict who kept the warden posted.'

Old Brocky took a soiled crumpled envelope from his pocket. 'I found this in Nelson's overalls pocket when I searched his room after he'd changed clothes and left.' He handed it to Pete. 'Nelson was supposed to give it to you, I reckon, but his plans backfired.'

Pete took the sheet of cheap paper from the envelope. Holding it towards the dim lamplight he read: '*Pete. Long Tom Savage and some other lifers are breakin' outa the pen on November 1st. Long Tom has a kid called*

Cottoneye in the reform school. A guard named Nelson is springin' Cottoneye out that same evenin'. I paid Nelson fifty bucks to spring you at the same time. You be ready and set to go. There'll be a horse and guns outside for you. Nelson knows where the hideout is. He'll take you and Cottoneye there. Mitch Moran is in on the big break. By God, you better show up.' The note was signed Booger Red.

Pete Craven tried to keep his voice steady as he handed the crudely written note back. 'Nelson and Cottoneye would have to drag me out that gate feet first.'

'I reckon they knew it, Pete.' Old Brocky grinned faintly. 'I wouldn't want to be in Nelson's boots when he meets Booger Red and has to fork over that fifty bucks.'

The wind-driven snow had clotted the steel-meshed window-panes. The banshee wail of the prison klaxons gave added sound to the fury of the blizzard that swept the Deer Lodge Valley.

Old Brocky walked to the telephone and cranked it. It took a while to get the connection through to the warden's office. Pete listened to the one-sided conversation until Old Brocky pronged the receiver on the hook.

'Three convicts surrendered,' he said. 'Two got shot down. Only one of the six got away—

the leader, Long Tom Savage. Nobody's picked up his trail, nor is there any trace of Nelson and Cottoneye or Booger Red.'

'Mitch?' questioned Pete, his voice unsteady.

'Mitch and his missus and daughter are on the train. They got off safely.' Old Brocky put his hand on the boy's shoulder. 'It'll be a long rough trail, Pete,' he said, 'but you stick it out here like you claim you will, and maybe you'll come out ahead.'

CHAPTER TEN

Little resemblance remained of Booger Red's whelp and the lean, hard six-foot cowhand who rode up out of the early summer sunset and through the far gate of the Bradded Z Ranch.

Zee Dunbar, sitting on the wide veranda in his wheelchair, lowered his field-glasses and shoved them into the leather case strapped to the wide arm. He slid a 30–40 box-magazine Winchester cavalry carbine from its saddle scabbard rigged along the chair's high back.

Zee was badly in need of a haircut and shave and a hot bath. The day had been warm and his shirt was dark with sweat. He stank of its staleness and the booze he had been drinking since sunrise, when he was wont to start his long daylight vigil, wheeling his chair up and down the porch for hours on end.

Zee had had the wide porch extended all around the house so that he could see whoever approached from any direction. Also he could follow the shade as the sun moved, or remain in the sun as it suited his restless surly moods.

Zee Dunbar had aged twenty years in a three-year duration contest of pain and hatred and bitterness, and a helpless crippled restlessness that seriously threatened the grizzled cowman's sanity. He averaged more than a quart of liquor a day now and bought it by the barrel. He was never quite sober night or day, nor was he ever so drunk that his faculties were impaired. He was still fast with a gun.

Zee Dunbar now thumbed the rear sight of the Winchester to the fifth notch. 'Stay away from the back of my chair, woman,' he growled at his wife, who had stepped out of the house to stand behind the chair. 'Stand out where I can see you, where you can't spin my chair around to spoil a man's aim like you did once.'

Tracy Dunbar moved from behind the wheel-chair and to the edge of the porch railing. Save for the hard etched tiny lines at the corners of her mouth and eyes, she had lost nothing of her youthful lines of exotic beauty. Her dark hair was plaited and coiled. Her body still retained a boyish slimness, with the small high breasts thrusting against a house-dress of faded blue gingham. A pair of Indian-tanned moccasins with blue bead work were on her small bare feet. Tracy still had the clean-cut thoroughbred look, until you saw the dark shadows under her eyes, until you looked into the eyes themselves. There you saw the marks of suffering and silent rebellion. There was no softness, no surrender to be discerned in their opaque, fathomless coldness.

Not even the loud explosion of the gun almost within arm's reach could disturb her poise.

Pete Craven heard the whine of the steel jacket bullet. His lips stretched back in a thin-lipped flat grin that matched his cold eyes. He reined up his horse. Shifting his weight to his left stirrup, he dropped his knotted bridle reins and reached for the sack of Bull Durham and book of cigarette papers in his shirt pocket.

'Keep your hands where I can watch 'em,' Zee Dunbar shouted loud enough for Pete to hear. 'Don't travel out of a walk.'

Pete twisted his cigarette into shape, licked

it and pulled a match head across his thumbnail. His hands were steady enough. Now that it was coming to a showdown of some kind, the knot had gone out of his belly. It had been there for a long time but was more of a nervous tension than fear.

It was Tracy, not Zee Dunbar, he dreaded meeting. He hadn't seen her since that night. When he saw her grip the wooden porch railing and lean a little forward, Pete knew she had recognized him.

'It's Pete Craven,' Pete heard her tell Zee, fear in her voice. But he was unprepared for it when he saw her step behind the wheel-chair and spin it around swiftly.

Pete's hand dropped to his six-shooter. He was fully prepared for some wild drunken outburst. Instead he heard Zee Dunbar's raucous laughter as he shoved the Winchester back into its scabbard. He had a bottle in his hand as the outburst of drunken laughter ceased as abruptly as it had begun, and he twisted the chair from the girl's grasp and wheeled himself to the edge of the porch.

'By God, you've grown into a man,' Zee said as Pete rode up. 'Step off, Pete. I'll have the barn man take your horse.'

Pete swung from the saddle slowly and dropped his bridle reins. He saw Tracy as she stood behind the wheelchair, her head held high, a fixed smile on her pale tight lips. There was a mixture of pleading and defiance in her shadowed eyes.

'Steve Costello,' Pete said, as he came up the porch steps, 'says I'm paroled into your custody. He said you'd explain why.'

'That's right,' Zee said, telling the boy to sit down.

Pete was remembering how Steve Costello, acting as the cowman's attorney, had seemed purposely vague as to Zee Dunbar's reason for having Pete paroled into his custody.

'Zee Dunbar stole your ranch,' the lawyer had said. 'He was the indirect cause of your killing a man. He wants to make atonement. Let it ride, Pete. If he's got an ace up his sleeve, we'll call the misdeal when he lays it on the table.'

They'd left it like that. Pete felt no fear as he faced the cowman now. Steve had told him that Zee hadn't drawn a sober breath since the night Pete saw him on the train and that he was quarrelsome and ugly.

A hint of a grim smile pulled the corners of Pete's mouth as the realization came that he possessed something that the cowman wanted. He knew things that Zee could only guess at, with the unanswered questions gnawing his insides like rat teeth for so long. Jealousy of his young wife had poisoned him. It showed in his eyes that asked questions he dare not put into words for fear he would get the truthful answers.

Pete lost all fear of the older man as he sensed the cowman's motive in sending for him. The knowledge must have showed in Pete's eyes because Zee leaned back from his tensed position and the strong square, blunt-fingered hands relaxed the grip on the bottle.

'Have you heard anything direct from Booger Red?' Zee Dunbar finally asked.

'No, sir,' Pete said. 'I broke with Booger Red that day at the ranch. All I want is for him to let me alone. Strictly alone.'

'Booger Red will never let you alone, Pete, till he's dead and in his grave. Even then there will be others to take it up where your old man left off.'

'Who?'

'A tough, tow-headed kid called Cottoneye Savage, to name only one,' Zee said. 'There's the pockmarked Nelson and Long Tom Savage and perhaps Lance Rader, all pardners of Booger Red,' he added.

Pete nodded without looking up.

'Me'n you is mixed up in this, Pete, and we better stick together. That's why I had you paroled to me.'

'I don't see where that will do us any good.' Pete looked up. 'I figured on drifting to some place where nobody knows me. That's what Mitch Moran did when he got out of the pen.'

'That's what Steve Costello told me you figured on doin'. Steve reckoned it was the only thing for you to do, but I changed his mind.' Zee leaned forward, gripping the bottle.

'Mitch Moran thought the same thing,' Zee went on. 'He changed his name time after time when he drifted from one new range to another. But there was always somebody showed up to call him Mitch Moran. It would be the same thing with Booger Red's kid.'

'Mitch?' Pete's throat was tight, his mouth dry when he voiced the question. 'Did they kill Mitch Moran?'

'No. Mitch Moran has a law badge pinned to his undershirt. He was a longs ways from dead last word I got. He's a stock detective workin' along the Wyoming-Montana border, lone-handed, buildin' up a rep as a bounty hunter for the Cattlemen's Association. Mitch left his wife and daughter where they'd be safe.'

It was news to Pete and he said so.

'But they're bound to get Mitch,' Pete said. 'The odds are too big. The law of averages will settle it.'

'Meanwhile he's dealin' 'em plenty misery,' Zee said. He took a drink and put the bottle in a pocket on the chair. 'I'm crippled,' he said bitterly. 'A man in a wheelchair can't run a cow outfit.'

'I heard Teal was running the Bradded Z,' Pete said bluntly.

Zee wheeled his chair close to Pete. 'I want you to run my outfit,' he said in a low tone. 'I need a man I can trust.'

Pete felt the blood pounding into the vein of his neck.

'What about Teal?' he asked.

'I reckon,' said Zee Dunbar, 'that will be the first job you'll have to tackle when you get around to it. But let Teal hang and rattle for a while. Teal has fired most of my old hands and hired a bunch of tough cowhands that's givin' the Bradded Z a hard rep. But those old hands will come back whenever I send 'em word that Teal don't ramrod the outfit no more. It'll take a little time before you're in shape to declare yourself.'

'Supper's ready.' At the sound of Tracy's voice Zee spun his chair around on one wheel.

Pete could not help but see the angry scowl that pulled the shaggy eyebrows together, the ugly glint of suspicion in the bloodshot pale eyes.

Tracy stood just behind the screen door, holding it open, her eyes smouldering with a strange mixture of hate and contempt and fear.

'How long have you been standin' there with your ears cocked, woman?' Zee's voice was a low growl, nasty in its implication.

A quick angry flush put colour into Tracy's cheeks as her upper lip curled back to show even white teeth. 'Shall I set an extra place for Pete Craven,' she asked, ignoring the cowman's accusation, 'or will he eat with the ranch hands?'

'Pete eats with me.' Zee wheeled past her into the hall. A new bedroom and adjoining bathroom had been added just beyond the entrance hall. Zee had to have a room on the ground floor. He had wheeled himself in there. His voice harsh and thick with suppressed anger and booze came from inside the bedroom.

'She'll show you where to wash up, Pete.' The door slammed shut, punctuating the words.

Pete noticed that the folding doors to the front parlour were closed. Tracy motioned him and he followed her through the dining-room. There was a clean white tablecloth on the round mahogany table. One place only was set at the supper table. Tracy held the swinging door to the kitchen open while Pete went through. The appetizing odour of sourdough came from the open oven door of the big kitchen range.

Tracy picked up a kettle from the stove and carried it out to the lean-to shed. She poured some hot water into a tin wash basin on a bench.

'I'll finish getting supper,' she said, 'while you wash up.'

Pete washed and was drying his face and hands on the roller towel when Tracy came back.

'For God's sake, be careful what you say,' she warned Pete. 'Watch Zee like you'd watch a vicious dog that should be chained or destroyed. Don't question anything you see here. Don't cross him in any way. Tonight, when he locks himself in his room, get away from this place if you have to walk. Keep going till you're off the Bradded Z range.'

Pete turned to face her. Her face was white as if powdered by alkali dust and her eyes were dark with dread.

'What made you come back here?' she asked tensely.

'I got paroled into Zee's custody.' Pete felt the contagion of her nameless dread. 'Didn't you know?' he asked.

'Who would tell me? Zee never speaks to me unless he gives an order. I do the squaw work. Sleep in the hired girl's room off the kitchen. Nobody's gone upstairs since the day

Zee came back crippled and brought me back to wait on him hand and foot. I haven't set foot beyond the gate, nor seen a woman in all that time. You are the first man I've been allowed to talk to and he has his own insane reasons for it. Get away tonight, before he kills you. I know what I'm talking about, Pete. You don't.'

'I'm here to stay,' Pete said stubbornly. 'Zee's hired me ...' He bit off the words. He had heard old Zee's door slam open, then his harsh voice saying, 'Fetch me a bottle, woman.'

'That's what he calls me.' She held out her ringless hands. There was no wedding ring there, no white circle on the tanned fingers to show that she had ever worn a wedding ring. 'Woman!' She smiled crookedly. 'I don't know if he divorced me or if I'm still his wedded wife. Not that it matters.' She gripped Pete's arm. 'Get away from here tonight, before it's too late. Zee knows a few things he's twisted around in his drunken brain, things he keeps secret, hoarding the ugly lies he's made up out of a warped mind. Kill him, Pete. Kill him, first chance you get. Before he kills you. Before he kills us both.' A dry sob caught in her throat.

Pete's hands took hold of her shoulders and he felt the tremble, saw the dark shadowed eyes misted by unshed tears. 'I'm not killing Zee,' he told her. 'I have to stay here, understand. I won't let him hurt you,' Pete whispered. He looked past her head, almost on a level with his, so close he felt her breath on his cheek, and saw Zee Dunbar in his chair in the doorway.

Pete saw the six-shooter gripped in the cowman's hand and the blued steel barrel pointed at Tracy's back, the ugly look in the bloodshot eyes. He heard the click of the gun hammer and shoved Tracy aside with a sudden violence that threw her off balance against the shed.

'Take it easy, Mister,' Pete said, his voice gritty. His right hand gripped the butt of the gun in its holster along his lean flank and his eyes were cold with menace.

The two men eyed one another in a long wordless scrutiny. Then Zee's gun barrel lowered and he let down the hammer, sliding the gun into its holster on the chair. A sort of stricken look filmed his eyes as he gripped the wire wheels and backed the chair away. A few moments later Pete heard Zee's bedroom door slam shut.

A choked sob came from Tracy who was crouched on the floor in the far corner of the lean-to. 'Kill him,' she whispered. 'Kill him before he kills you!'

'Zee had his chance,' Pete said tonelessly, 'to kill us both. But he changed his mind. He won't kill either one of us till he's finished using us. I'm playing my string out here.'

'What are you trying to prove?' Tracy had recovered some of her poise. She had shaken off the fear with a visible effort. Her voice sounded brittle and her eyes probed his as she moved closer.

'I'll prove something,' Pete told her, 'if I live that long.'

Tracy's hand reached out suddenly, gripping his wrist. Her eyes were cold and wary now. 'Just what is it you expect to find out?' she asked, a strange tenseness in her voice that came from taut nerves. 'You and that drunken Zee Dunbar?' Her upper lip pulled back.

Pete Craven looked at her as if seeing her for the first time. The grip of her strong cold fingers like handcuffs on his wrist, the fury and suspicion in her eyes, the brittle tone of her voice, brought back some vague memory.

'How much have you told that filthy crippled brute?' Her quick breathing touched his face. 'What did you tell that lawyer, Steve Costello? Judge Dewar? You murdered a law officer. You should be in the pen but you got off with a few years in reform school. Now you come sneaking back here under the protective custody of a drunken insane sadistic cripple, who should be in a padded cell in the insane asylum at Warm Springs.' Her voice shrilled.

Pete stared into her eyes, an empty cold feeling inside him. A few minutes ago he had felt sorry for her. Perhaps he had saved her life by flinging her aside. He had killed a man with the gun she had put in his hand. If she had taken the witness stand and told the truth, he would have been cleared. He had been a kid then, cowed by his old man's quirtings. An awkward country boy unused to the ways of a woman, enamoured by her attentions. The entire panoramic picture of it all came back with a sickening clarity as his searching gaze tried to probe beneath the surface of her eyes.

'You spill your guts,' Tracy's voice came from behind clenched teeth, 'about Lance Rader showing up that night?'

'No,' Pete said, his voice cold. 'I've never told anybody anything that happened the night I killed big Jim West with the gun you handed me. I intend to keep my mouth shut. But from here on you and your husband will settle your own family quarrels.' Pete twisted his wrist free from her fingers.

'I'm warning you for the last time,' Tracy said. 'Leave this place tonight and don't ever come back.'

'That has the sound of a threat, lady.'

'It is more than a threat. You'll find it backed up. But it'll be too late to run then. The time to run for it is right now.'

Pete Craven looked out into the gathering dusk.

Tracy, mistaking it, whispered as she stood close behind him. 'There is a fresh horse in the barn. It's getting too late for Zee to line his gun-sights.'

Pete turned and brushed past her. He walked through the kitchen and into the dining-room. Zee had lighted the lamp and was seated in his wheel-chair at the table.

'Pull up a chair, Pete. There's whisky in the decanter. Pour yourself a drink. You look like you needed a big 'un,' Zee said.

Pete shook his head, a forced grin on his face. 'I'd only puke it up.'

'She'll be in with the grub directly.' Zee spoke as if he had forgotten what had happened and Pete was willing to go along with the notion. He pulled up his chair and sat down.

'From what Steve Costello tells me,' Zee was saying 'that Slade Farm Old Brocky's got is actually something to be proud of. It got a big write-up in the newspapers. Steve says you did a good job getting it organized.'

'I tried to make a hand,' Pete said.
'What do you think of Doc Cole, Pete?'
'Doc's a top hand, sir.'
'He drinks a lot, from what I hear.'
'No, sir,' Pete said quickly. 'I never saw Doc drunk. He never makes a mistake.'
'I got a .45 slug lodged against my spine. The Butte doctors were scared to dig it out. Said I'd die on the table. It gives me unholy hell twenty-four hours a day. Sometimes when whisky won't kill the pain I take a morphine pill, but not till I can't stand it no longer. I don't want to wind up with dope. Whisky's bad enough.' Zee took a big swallow from his whisky glass and grinned.

'When we get the Bradded Z straightened out I'm going to let Doc Cole try his luck,' he added.

Tracy came in with a long meat platter balanced in each hand. She wore a white apron over her shapeless squaw dress. She put the platters on the table and set a place for Pete without looking at the two men. She brought in covered dishes of vegetables, then two cups of coffee.

They ate in silence. Pete discovered he was hungry. There was nothing left of his big steak but the T bone. The bowl of succotash was almost empty. Pete drank half a dozen cups of coffee and managed to consume a large wedge of apple pie.

Zee wheeled his chair into a small den he called the smoking-room. They sat and smoked while Pete told him about his first days at the reform school, about little Stub Slade who had never been on a horse. The crippled cowman, who had prompted Pete into telling the story, proved to be a good listener.

'Stub Slade had guts, sir,' Pete finished.

'Forget that sir handle, Pete. Call me Zee.' He grinned faintly. 'Speakin' of guts. You got your share, Pete. It takes a man with plenty guts to look into a gun barrel. That's the first time ol' Zee Dunbar ever thumbed back a gun hammer without pullin' the trigger. Sometime I might tell you why.' He spun his chair around and opened the closed door with a swift jerk, flinging it wide.

The shaft of light from the lamp on the table filtered into the hall. Pete sucked in his breath when he saw Tracy trapped by the dim glow where she had been crouched close to the door, eavesdropping.

There was a long painful moment of hushed silence. There was a look of sly crafty cunning on the cowman's face with its greying stubble of beard.

'Open the doors to the front parlour, woman,' Zee said, a grin twisting his lips.

'Light the big lamp. Crank up that talkin' machine and start the music. Put on somethin' fancy to dance in. Get movin', woman.' Zee closed the door and spun the chair around.

'I reckon you didn't do much dancin' at reform school, eh, Pete?' The twisted grin left his eyes cold, wary.

'No,' Pete said stiffly. 'I never was much of a hand at dancin'.'

'Get her to show you the latest steps she picked up with Lance Rader at the Butte dance-halls.' Zee splashed whisky into a tall glass and gulped it down. 'I ain't seen any of the tricks that range dude taught her. I been holdin' off thinkin' he might show up. Dancin's her speciality.' Zee took another swallow of whisky.

Pete felt the cold sweat beading out under his eyes. The palms of his clenched hands were slimy as he gripped his chair. 'I don't feel like showin' off my awkwardness, Zee, if it's all the same to you,' Pete managed to say.

'Supposin' we leave it up to her, Pete.' There was a quiet menace in the tone of his voice as he backed the wheel-chair around and out the door.

There was nothing left for Pete to do but follow.

CHAPTER ELEVEN

No butterfly escaped from its drab cocoon was ever more beautiful than Tracy Dunbar in her low cut, sleeveless gown of glove-fitting scarlet silk and French-heeled silver slippers, with her sleek black hair coiled like a crown on her head, her green eyes smudged by long black lashes, deep set under heavy black brows, the pallor of her skin adding the last exotic touch to her beauty as she made her entrance.

Anticipating the cowman's thoughts that prompted this torturous ugly farce, she chose a waltz recording. At the first strains of the 'Blue Danube' waltz, Tracy curtsied, head lowered, red lips fixed in a painted smile.

'Cinderella at the ball,' her vibrant voice fell across the strains of the muted violins. Then she walked over to where Pete Craven was standing beside the wheel-chair.

'The Prince Charming,' the painted smile left her eyes cold, green as winter ice, 'is too modest and bashful, therefore, Cinderella claims the honour of this waltz.'

Tracy was surpassing her woman's courage. Pete met it with a false gallantry as he forced a grin.

'You don't know what you're letting yourself in for, lady,' Pete said a little grimly.

Tracy came close into his arms, leading him with the tight cold pressure of her hand in his and her bare arm that went up across his shoulders. Her hair brushed his cheek, her whispered words were breathed into his ear. 'We'll give the sadistic brute more than he's bargained for. Hold me tight like a lover holds his woman. I'm yours tonight for the taking.'

Pete felt the brush of her lips against his cheek as she pressed close to him, guiding every movement of his lean hard body with hers. He could feel the pressure of her quick breathing in the thrust of her small breasts against him. The hand gripping his was no longer cold as it pulsed warmly in time to the violins. Her fingers crept up between his shoulder-blades, into the crisp thick wiry hair at the back of his head. As they moved slowly past the crippled cowman in the wheel-chair, Pete cut him a glancing look.

Zee Dunbar's stubbled face had a greyish sick pallor under the weathered crust. Pete faltered as he saw the twisted stricken look on Zee's tortured face. Tracy pulled him up like a rider pulls up a horse that's stumbled. 'Hold me,' the whispered words hissed. Pete felt the sharp quick pain as her teeth bit into the lobe of his ear.

The heavy pounding on the barred front door slammed through the music. Pete stopped in his tracks, twisting his head around quickly, his arm still around Tracy's slim waist.

He saw Zee spin his chair with one hand, the long-barrelled Colt gun in his other hand as he wheeled through the door.

Tracy had twisted free and was gone.

'Get out of here, Pete,' Zee's harsh whisper grated from the dark hallway. 'Pull the parlour doors shut.'

Pete's gun was in his hand as he moved. He pulled the folding doors together, leaving the hall dark. Zee's wheelchair was along the wall behind the front door. When the pounding on the door stopped, Zee's saw-edge voice lifted.

'Who the hell's making that racket?'

'Teal,' the reply came as a muffled sound through the door. 'Who else was you expectin', Zee?'

Pete Craven, crouched in behind the newel post in the darkness, with a gun in his hand, was reminded of another night.

'What in hell fetches you here, this hour of night, Teal? I thought your outfit was camped on the river.'

'I got news that can't be bellered from hell to breakfast, Zee. Open the door and let me in.'

'Who's with you, Teal?' Zee had wheeled his chair to the curtained hall window and was peering out into the moonlight.

'I'm alone,' Teal spoke sharply. 'I heard music inside. Lights showed behind the blinds in the front parlour. I wondered what the hell was goin' on here.'

'There's a closet under the stairway, Pete,' Zee whispered, wheeling his chair close. 'Get in there and stay hid till I tell you to come out. Leave the door open a crack so you can see.' The wheel-chair moved towards the door.

Zee slid the lock back and swung his chair in behind the door.

'Light a match, Teal,' called Zee. 'Hold it in both hands when you come in. The door's unlocked.'

'Don't get quick-triggered, Zee,' Teal said. A match flared and he held the flame cupped shoulder high as he came in. 'You act like you don't trust a man.'

'You're right, I don't,' Zee said. 'Open the doors to the parlour and make yourself at home, Teal.'

Zee wheeled his chair sideways against the door to close it, fastened the lock, and followed Teal.

Pete's gun was gripped as he watched Teal open the doors and walk across the empty room to where a whisky decanter and glasses were on a side table. Teal's back was towards the door as he pulled the ornate stopper from the decanter, bending his head to smell the aroma of twelve-year-old Bourbon whisky.

Teal turned around, his beady black eyes glinting as he eyed the gun in the hand of the crippled cowman.

Teal hadn't changed much, Pete thought, since the last time he'd seen him. The beady black eyes had the same opaque glint, the lipless mouth had lost nothing of its cruelty, the hatchet face with the sharp etched lines betrayed the same cunning, the straight coarse black hair without a single grey hair to show for the hard years had the same stove-polished look of being dyed. Teal's appearance had not undergone any change, save in Pete Craven's eyes that saw the killer now with adult eyes.

Pete, standing back in the dark closet, his gun ready, had lost something of his boy's fear and awe of the hired killer who was now ramrod of the big Bradded Z outfit. Here was the man Pete would have to get rid of if he played his string out with Zee Dunbar.

So long as he stayed hidden in the dark hallway Pete had the advantage if it came to a showdown. He couldn't see Zee because the high back of the wheel-chair concealed him. But Teal was in plain sight as he gulped his drink and set the empty glass and whisky bottle back on the table. He hooked his thumbs into the filled cartridge belt that slanted across his lean flanks and Pete saw that his right hand was within inches of the butt of his six-shooter in an open holster tied down on his thigh.

'What's on your mind, Teal?' Zee Dunbar's harsh voice shattered the uneasy quiet.

Teal replaced the stopper in the whisky decanter with studied care. His lipless mouth spread in a mirthless grin when he said, 'Why any man in his right mind wants to swill rotgut till he pukes is somethin' I never could figger out. It's rank poison.'

Teal took a sack of tobacco and book of papers from the pocket of his black sateen shirt and twisted a thin cigarette into shape, then lit it.

'You ride thirty miles to make a damn temperance speech, Teal?'

'Hell, no,' Teal said. 'I was just makin' conversation till you put that smokepole away.'

Zee made a chuckling sound as he shoved the long-barrelled Colt frontier gun into its holster rigged to the arm of the wheel-chair. 'Let's have the news, Teal!'

'There's a big drive of cattle on the way. Two thousand head of two-year-olds in the Question Mark road iron.' Teal's beady eyes glinted through tobacco smoke.

'I already got twenty-five hundred head, according to your count, that got dumped on my range and wintered on my hay. The Cattle Rustlers' Syndicate better find another dumping ground for their stolen cattle.' Zee spoke coldly.

Teal took a final drag and stubbed out the tiny butt against the wide lip of a large brass cuspidor.

'The Cattle Rustlers' Syndicate have worn out their welcome in Wyoming, Zee. They're on the run.'

'Maybe I better hand out a cryin' towel.' Zee leaned forward, his hands gripping the hard rubber tires, his eyes congested. He growled, 'I've been crowded as far as I go, Teal. Understand?'

Teal pushed back the dust and sweat-stained Stetson from his forehead that showed white in contrast to his weathered face.

'Two thousand head in the drive that's comin'. Twenty-five hundred already on your ranges. Forty-five hundred head of prime steers all told. At the rock bottom price of fifteen dollars a round, it amounts to sixty-seven thousand five hundred dollars. They want the long green laid on the barrel head.' Teal grinned crookedly as Zee spun his wheelchair in a tight circle.

'I might as well tell you that Booger Red Craven is head of the Syndicate and he's crowded hard,' Teal said. 'He'll settle for ten dollars a round.'

Zee bared his teeth. 'Booger Red Craven will settle for a damn sight less than that. I get my cartridges wholesale and it won't take but a cardboard box or two to pay off Booger Red and his Cattle Rustlers' Syndicate, down to the last two-bit renegade.' Zee spun the chair around and slid to a halt in the opening of the parlour folding doors. 'That goes as she lays, Teal.'

Teal's short laugh had an ugly sound as he hitched up his cartridge belt, the thumb of his right hand on the hammer of his gun. 'Looks to me, Zee, like you bit off a big hunk of bear meat. The more you chaw, the bigger it swells in your mouth till you can't spit the tough wad out and you can't swallow it. You'll choke down and die after a while. You talk too big for a wheel-chair cripple, Zee.' Teal's beady eyes seemed to shrink smaller until the opaque black glowed like twin red coals in the lamplight.

'You're supposed to be ramrodding my Bradded Z outfit, Teal. That's a hell of a way to look after a crippled man's interests,' Zee Dunbar said quietly.

A dark flush came into Teal's hatchet face.

He said, 'Maybe Booger Red's Cattle Rustlers' Syndicate's got me over the barrel.'

An ugly grin twisted Zee's whiskered face as he shook his head from side to side slowly. 'Booger Red and his outfit are on the run. They're in no shape to lay nobody across the barrel.' Zee leaned forward again. 'If I was to pay you the money you came here to collect, Booger Red and his renegades wouldn't see a dollar of it. From where I'm setting crippled, it looks like Teal wants a South America Stake.' Zee took a filled quart bottle from a leather pouch on the chair and twisted the cork out, taking a long drink.

'You always was a hard man to shave, Zee,' Teal said. 'A hard man to lie to and make it stick.' His beady eyes fixed on the bottle in Zee's hand.

'Then spread your soogans, Teal,' Zee said bluntly.

Teal pulled a long narrow printed form from his pocket. 'This is a bench warrant with the name Teal written on it. I found it tacked to the cabin door at the Craven place where I was camped. It's a copy of an old indictment that ran me out of Wyoming. If I'm picked up alive, I'll hang.' Teal tossed it across the room into Zee's lap. 'You keep a lot of money locked up in your safe in the smokin'-room here. I need about fifty thousand for that boat trip, Zee. I aim to get it.' Teal's gun was in his hand.

Pete Craven was sweating inside the dark closet. Things were shaping up for the climax. Zee had been playing Teal like a fisherman plays a trout.

'About this big drive of cattle Booger Red's fetchin' up,' Zee spoke. 'Was you lyin' about that, Teal?'

'Hell, no. He sent Long Tom Savage's kid, Cottoneye, with the message to have the money laid on the line when he crossed the herd at the Craven place on the Missouri River.' Teal wet his dry lips as he eyed the whisky bottle. 'I sent word back that the long green would be there.'

'Maybe I can have this indictment squashed,' Zee slapped the bench warrant against the bottle, 'if you'll follow my orders; when the gunsmoke's drifted clear, maybe you can have your South America stake, providing you get the job done to suit me.'

'I got a gun pointed at your belly, Zee,' Teal said. 'You wouldn't be talkin' yourself out of a tight?' Teal's lipless mouth skinned back.

'No.' Zee wheeled his chair away from the door opening. 'You'd be dead before you got your gun hammer thumbed back. You've been covered from the time you stepped in the front door. Looks like it's your turn to put up the smokepole, Teal. I'm runnin' no whizzer so don't crowd your bad luck.'

Teal was white around the mouth as he slid his six-shooter into its holster.

Pete Craven walked out of the closet, his gun in his hand. He watched Teal like a hawk as he stepped into the lighted room.

It took a long moment for Teal to recognize him. Pete had changed from a gangling awkward, cowed kid into a six-foot man with the build and lithe co-ordination of a middleweight. Pete's broken nose had been badly set and a layer of scar-tissue gave his heavy black eyebrows a beetling appearance. There was a man's set to the corner of his mouth and his grey eyes were cold with suspicion as he stood there with the gun in his hand.

Teal spilled tobacco into a paper and rolled it into a cigarette. 'Booger Red's kid growed into somethin' mansize,' he said. He pulled a match-head across his thumbnail and his hand was steady as it cupped the flame. 'What's he doin' here, Zee?' The question came out in drifting smoke.

'I had Pete Craven paroled into my custody, Teal.' A grin crossed the cowman's face. He corked the bottle and slid it back into the leather pouch. His hand held the six-shooter when it came into sight.

'You had it made to kill me, Teal.' Zee's voice had turned menacing. 'You aimed to murder a cripple and rob my safe when you came here tonight.' Zee spoke to Pete without taking his eyes from Teal. 'You can put up your gun, Pete. I got the deal.'

But Pete kept the gun in his hand. There was no telling what the cowman had in his warped mind.

'I had that bench warrant sworn out, Teal,' Zee told him. 'I had the law man tack it to the cabin door at the Craven place where you'd be bound to find it.'

'Are you tryin' to crowd me into gun play, Zee?' Teal asked. No trace of fear showed in his beady eyes as he spat the short stub of cigarette from the corner of his mouth into the cuspidor. 'Or do you expect me to go down on my knees and beg for mercy? Either way you're wastin' your whisky-stinking breath.'

'The idea was to throw a scare into you, Teal. Smoke you out. And it worked. Did you get word to your side-pardner, Lance Rader, that you aimed to kill me and rob the safe?' Zee asked harshly.

Teal made no reply to the accusation, one way or the other. His poker face and beady eyes revealed nothing.

'Maybe you dealt Rader out, figgerin' you'd earned it all when you killed ol' Zee Dunbar.

Purty Lance would marry the widow and get hold of the Bradded Z for his share of the deal you two been cookin' up on a slow fire. That the size of it, Teal?'

'Figger it out to suit yourself, Zee,' Teal said flatly. 'Your whisky talk is gettin' wearisome. You said somethin' about squashin' that old indictment. Get down to cases.'

'I got word that you've paid off your tough cowhands,' Zee said.

'All but the horse wrangler and cook,' Teal said. 'Your remuda and chuck wagon are on the way to the home ranch. The spring calf round-up is over.' Teal reached into the pocket of his denim jacket.

'Hold it!' The double-click of Zee's gun hammer made a loud noise. 'Don't pull a sneak gun, if that's what you had in mind, Teal.'

Teal's hand came out with a small vest pocket-sized book. He tossed it into Zee's lap. 'There's the calf tally book,' he said, then added, 'quit tryin' to throw a scare into me, Zee. You won't kill me if you can use me. Let's get to the point.'

'Fetch Lance Rader here on the hoof, Teal,' Zee slapped the bench warrant against his chair, 'and I'll burn this thing. That's it. Take it or leave it.'

'It's a deal,' Teal answered. 'What about the money?'

'You'll get paid when you get the job done.'

'What about this trail herd?' Teal asked. 'How you aim to deal with the Cattle Rustlers' Syndicate?'

'I'm dealin' with one of 'em now, Teal. You and Lance Rader are the Cattle Rustlers' Syndicate. Booger Red and the rest of the Question Mark outfit are no more than hired hands.'

The eyes of the two men met and held for a long time.

'How long have you known it, Zee?'

'Long enough to have the wolf-trap set. Set and baited, Teal.' Zee's eyes were mean. 'The wolf-trap set and baited,' he repeated.

'What did you use for bait?' Teal asked warily.

'My wife.' Zee spat the words out like a dirty taste that had been in his mouth for a long, long time. 'Get out, you son of a bitch!'

Teal's hands were lifted to shoulder height as he backed away from the crippled cowman and the seared look in his bloodshot eyes, away from the cocked gun.

Pete followed Teal to the door, his gun in his hand. When he walked out without a backward glance, Pete closed the door and locked it. Then he heard the sharp, hissing intake of breath and the soft rustling of skirts and the barely audible sound of silk-stockinged feet on the carpeted floor of the hall. He caught a brief glimpse of Tracy's shadowy form before it disappeared.

Pete gave a start and ran into the parlour as a loud crashing filled the room. He saw the heavy quirt in Zee's hand as it slashed at the ornate morning glory horn of the Victor Talking machine, upsetting the machine from its stand. The crippled cowman was cursing thickly with drunken maniacal fury as he ran his wheel-chair over the wreckage on the floor, back and forth, spinning the chair in tight circles, flattening the painted horn into a shapeless thing, the waxed records crunching under the hard rubber-tired wheels.

Pete paused in the doorway, awed by the crazed fury of the crippled cowman. His shaggy grey hair was a sweat dank tangle above his livid face with its stubble of whiskers, the bloodshot eyes congested, filmed with a blind, sightless hate. The heavy quirt hung by its loop from the thick wrist as Zee clawed for his six-shooter, his other hand twisting the big wheel of his chair. The heavy gun slid away from his sweaty grip, falling to the floor. Zee strained forward, his arm outstretched to pick up the gun, the sudden shift of his weight toppling the chair forward, pitching him out. Zee fell with a dull crash, the chair coming down on his back with the unchecked force of his weight. A harsh animal scream of mortal agony came from under the wreckage as the wheels of the overturned chair spun slowly and then stopped.

Pete Craven stood rooted to his tracks, his gun still in his hand. Tracy's low whimper behind him in the shadows sounded through the last echo of Zee's agonized moan.

'He's dead.' Pete heard the harsh whisper behind him. He could feel Tracy's arm tightly. 'Dead, understand! Dead!' Her high-pitched keening laugh pierced his eardrum, then choked in a dry sob.

Pete had to brace himself, holster his gun, to take hold of her. Tracy's slim body went tense, rigid, trembling in its tautness as he held her shoulders in a tight grip.

The jangling ring of the wall telephone crashed through her hysterical laughter. Its persistent ringing within arm's reach penetrated and the shrill laughter broke off.

'Answer it,' Tracy whispered fearfully.

'That you, Zee?' A man's voice answered Pete's guarded 'Hello.'

'No,' Pete said clearing his tight throat. 'This is Pete.'

'It's Steve Costello, Pete. Everything all

right? Where's Zee?'

'I think Zee might be dead, Steve,' Pete managed to say.

'Good God! You shot Zee?'

'No,' Pete said. 'I didn't shoot him. Zee fell out of his wheel-chair. It came over on top of him. It just happened. I haven't had time to look at him yet.'

'Where's Tracy?'

'She kinda went into hysterics,' Pete told him. 'She's comin' out of it now. Better send a doctor out.'

'I'll get Doc Cole out there. He's here with me now. Don't try to move Zee till we get there.' Steve paused a moment, then said, 'Is there anything you want to tell me before I hang up, Pete?' His voice was guarded.

Pete thought fast, then said, 'Teal showed up. There was a showdown. Zee wants me to run his outfit. I'm here alone. If Teal comes back I'll have to shoot first. If Teal comes back with Lance Rader, there'll be two of 'em.'

'Hold on tight till we get there, Pete. I'll bring you a man to even the odds.' Steve hung up.

Tracy was sitting crouched on the horsehair sofa when Pete went into the parlour. Her eyes were still glazed. Pete motioned her back as he crossed the room. 'Stay where you are,' he told her.

Pete lifted the wheel-chair cautiously and rolled it back out of the way. Then he squatted alongside the cowman, who lay sprawled on his back. There was a grey pallor to his weathered skin. Pete found the uneven beat of his pulse. Zee's breathing was shallow.

Tracy came over and bending down she wiped the film of sweat from Zee's face and forehead with a handkerchief. Pete told her that Steve Costello was bringing a doctor out, that they were not supposed to move Zee.

Tracy picked up Zee's six-shooter. When he looked up her eyes were green as bottle glass.

'If Teal comes back with Lance Rader,' Tracy's voice was as cold as her eyes, 'you take Teal. I'll tend to Rader. With my husband's gun.' She laid the six-shooter on the littered carpet beside her, and wiped more sweat from Zee's face.

Pete, looking into Zee's grey face, thought he detected a faint sardonic grin on his mouth.

CHAPTER TWELVE

Pete Craven brought a basin of warm water from the bathroom, a large sponge and clean towel, motioning Tracy back to the sofa. She took Zee's six-shooter with her.

Pete was sponging the cowman's face and head when Zee Dunbar squinted his bloodshot pale eyes open.

'Roll me over, Pete,' Zee forced the words out from behind clenched teeth. 'Pull up my shirt and feel around till you locate a knot, about the size of a walnut along the backbone. Slit the skin with your jack-knife and I think the slug will pop out from the way it feels. Have at it, son. It'll relieve the pain.' The eyelids closed as if the cowman had used his final strength.

'Steve Costello is bringing Doc Cole out. They should be here before long. Steve telephoned right after your accident.'

'Accident?' Zee's shaggy brows knitted in puzzlement. 'I don't recollect no accident. I remember running Teal off. What happened after that?'

'You were charging around in your wheelchair, cutting didos. It turned over on top of you.'

'Hell of a note.' The cowman's lips twisted. 'Getting bucked off a gentle-broke wheelchair. Hell of a way for an old cowhand to wind up; throwed by a damned wheelchair.' Zee's puckered eyes swivelled till they found Tracy sitting on the edge of the sofa, the gun gripped in both hands.

Tracy's darkened eyes met Zee's fixed scrutiny without flinching. A grin forced itself across the cowman's stubbled face and his eyes came back to Pete.

'Let's see what a shot of booze will do for me,' he said, closing his eyes tight, to shut out something he had seen in that long moment when Tracy's eyes met his and held.

Zee had drained the glass of whisky that Pete held to the stiff lips when the rattle of buckboard wheels sounded outside.

Pete had lit the swinging lamp in the hall. He unlocked the door and opened it. It was just getting daylight as Doctor Cole stepped up on the porch. Steve Costello and a veiled woman in a grey tailored suit were getting out of the rig at the hitchrack. Two mounted men were riding up out of the early dawn.

'I brought a nurse,' Cole said as he gripped Pete's hand. 'I'll find my way in. You take care of the nurse and Steve Costello.'

The lawyer was dressed in riding breeches and English boots and a corduroy Norfolk jacket. The bulge of a pistol in a shoulder holster showed under the coat. He had an arm across the shoulders of the nurse as they approached the house.

Pete Craven came across the porch and cleared the steps as the nurse lifted the veil from her face.

'Nora!' Pete stumbled a little.

Steve gave a little push that sent Nora towards him as Pete caught his balance.

As Pete held her in his arms his legs trembled and there was a tightness in his throat as a warmth thawed the hardness inside him. Nora's hat and veil had fallen off, and her mop of curly brown hair was tucked under his shoulder. As he kissed her, her lips moved soundlessly against his mouth and he knew the meaning of their wordless message.

Pete was still holding Nora when Sheriff Ike Niber and the man with him pulled up and swung to the ground.

It had been a long eight years or more since Pete had seen the short, stocky, bow-legged Mitch Moran. His boyhood recollection of the man had been a sunburnt, square-jawed face, with a grin and a humorous twinkle in his eyes like he was enjoying a joke he had played on somebody. Mitch's laugh in those days had been infectious.

Now the grimace that twisted the scar-ridged face was a terrible mocking of the Irishman's smile, the glint in the eyes under scarred brows a ghostly relic of that remembered twinkle.

Nora pulled Pete's head down and whispered in his ear, 'They cut his tongue out,

Pete. He can't talk. I'll tell you about it later.'

Pete felt the grip of Mitch Moran's callused hand as his free arm went across his daughter's shoulders.

'Mitch and I'll take care of the horses, Pete. You take Nora's suitcase in,' the tall raw-boned sheriff said. 'What shape's Zee in?'

'Bad,' Pete said.

'Better get in there, Nora,' Sheriff Ike told the girl, 'in case Doc wants to operate right away.'

Pete took the suitcase and he and Nora went up the steps. The shock of Mitch Moran's scarred face had chilled Pete's guts.

Tracy opened the front door for them. She said that Doctor Cole had decided to operate right away. He'd use the kitchen table.

Stripped to a sleeveless undershirt and pants, Doctor Cole was scrubbing his hands and arms as Nora came into the kitchen. She had changed quickly to a white uniform.

While the doctor sorted out whatever surgical instruments he would need, Nora dropped them into an open pot of boiling water. She scrubbed the large kitchen table and laid out the sterilized instruments on a cloth on a side table.

'What are Zee's chances?' Pete asked the doctor.

'Double the odds that Butte surgeons gave

him,' Doctor Cole said. 'I wouldn't touch it but Zee Dunbar says to go ahead, that he'd rather be dead than the way he is now. He'd already sent for me and told Steve Costello to pilot me to the ranch. That's how come I happen to be here now when I'm badly needed.'

Zee's eyes squinted open when they moved him on an improvised stretcher. There was a forced grin on his stubbled face, when he said, 'Have at it, Doc.'

While Doctor Cole and Nora Moran worked over the cowman on the kitchen table, the others sat in the front parlour to wait.

Pete tried to avoid looking at Mitch Moran's scarred face and the look of worried fear that darkened Tracy Dunbar's green eyes as she sat with clenched hands. She looked like she wanted to run away but some sort of defiant pride was holding her here to face her enemies. She had changed into a plain cotton dress and her face was pale in the dim light of the room.

Steve Costello crossed the room and sat down beside Tracy. He put an arm across her shoulder.

'If Zee Dunbar dies,' he said, 'there is nobody to blame for his death but himself. I was closer to him than any man. I know the truth behind Zee's actions.'

Tracy's eyes looked into his, waiting for some sort of explanation.

'As Zee's attorney,' Steve Costello said, 'I could have prevented the shooting scrape at Butte. I got drunk with him on the train. I could have dropped a couple of sleeping pills into his drinks and he would have been in a drunken stupor when we reached Butte. As Zee's counsellor that would have come under the code of ethics. But I had every reason in the world to hate Zee Dunbar's guts. He was well aware of it when he hired me. After I had accepted his retainer fee, Zee taunted me with every drink we took from his bottle.' A thin smile crossed the handsome face. 'You are probably thinking you are to blame, Tracy, for the bullet in Zee Dunbar's back that may well cause his death. But if we go into self-accusation, there is nobody to blame for Zee's death, if he dies, but Steve Costello.'

Sheriff Ike Niber had found a pack of cards. He and Mitch Moran were playing a game of Seven-up.

Steve Costello got up and told Tracy and Pete to follow him. He led the way into the smoking-room.

Tracy had taken hold of Pete's hand. 'I hated that man,' she whispered, 'up until now. I'm going to tell him the truth, Pete, about the killing of Jim West.'

Pete shook his head. 'There's no need of it. Not now, anyhow. Not tonight. I wish you'd quit blaming yourself, Tracy.'

'I'm glad you don't hate me, Pete. Everyone else does.'

'You've had a tough break, that's all,' Pete said kindly.

When the three of them were seated in the smoking-room, Steve Costello broke the silence.

'You're wondering about Mitch Moran's scarred face, Pete, so I'll explain how it happened.' Steve lit a long Virginia cheroot before he told the story.

'Mitch's wife had an excellent job waiting for her in the diet kitchen of the hospital at Denver, Colorado. Nora had made arrangements to enroll as a student nurse. Mitch was to travel as far as Denver with them and there they'd separate and live apart until it was safe for them to reunite. They boarded the train the night Mitch was paroled and travelled in a locked stateroom. But Mitch made the mistake of leaving the stateroom when the train stopped at a small town near the Wyoming border. He never returned.

'There were five other passengers aboard that same train that night,' Steve Costello continued talking. 'Booger Red Craven and Lance Rader were riding the cushions in the day coach. Long Tom and Cottoneye and Nelson, the pockmarked guard, rode the blind baggage. They'd managed somehow against great odds to make the ride to Fort Belknap and board the train there.

'Months ahead they'd planned to hold up the train when it reached Rawlings, Wyoming, but they'd held out that bit of information on Mitch Moran for some reason.

'They must have got a good laugh out of it when they were safely aboard and the train pulled out, with the prison searchlights and the alarm sounding the length of the Deer Lodge Valley, knowing the law would never suspect they'd try to make the long ride to the railway in the worst blizzard in history, let alone have the nerve to board a train.

'Nelson and Long Tom and Cottoneye Savage nearly froze to death in the cramped confines of the blind baggage, an outside position with meagre shelter from the small-end vestibule of the baggage car.

'The train hold-up failed for that reason. Booger Red and Lance Rader were kept busy for a while thawing the three men out and nursing them back to life. Booger Red had caught a brief glimpse of Mitch Moran when he got off the train at a wayside station for some fresh air. At the point of a gun he forced him into the day coach and when they left the train at Rawlings, Wyoming, they took Mitch with them. His wife and daughter went on to Denver without him.

'They worked Mitch over with knives and left him for dead in a bloody snowbank in an alley. A cop on his beat found him before he froze to death. Mitch was sent to the hospital at Denver and Nora nursed her father back to life, scarred and tongueless.'

The door opened then. Doctor Cole in his blood-splattered white gown, the strain of the ordeal showing in his eyes and his ruddy, sweaty face, came into the smoking-room.

'All Zee asked for,' the doctor wheezed, 'was the fighting chance I gave him. Zee Dunbar will be riding broncs in two weeks.'

A choked sob was torn from Tracy's throat as she slumped over in a dead, exhausted faint.

CHAPTER THIRTEEN

Sheriff Ike Niber told Pete Craven when they were alone later in the day, that Zee Dunbar had made a bad mistake when he forced the showdown with Teal. He'd sprung the trap they'd set to catch every renegade in the Cattle Rustlers' Syndicate.

He told how Mitch Moran had been the range detective who had run Booger Red and his outfit out of Wyoming. He'd smoked them out from the Hole-in-the-Wall country and they'd made a quick gatherment of cattle they'd already branded in the Question Mark road iron. Booger Red had sent word to Teal that the cattle were on the way and to have the money on hand for the pay-off when he took delivery of the stolen cattle some time next week or the week after, when they crossed the Missouri River at the old Craven place.

'I told Zee to string along with Teal,' the sheriff said. 'I told him to belly-ache and chaw the price down but to lay the dough on the line. I don't know what in hell got into Zee to blow up like he did. He sure made a batterass of the deal.'

'Zee wasn't himself when Teal showed up,' Pete told the sheriff. 'He was drunk and ornery. He got Teal by the short hairs and went to work. Had Teal sweatin' blood over that bench warrant before he ran him off.'

'Zee should have killed Teal when he had him dead to rights,' Sheriff Ike Niber said. 'As it is he'll get word to his pardner Lance Rader and Booger Red. Months of careful planning and conniving has been thrown away.' The big raw-boned sheriff seemed fit to be tied.

'Mitch Moran should have left that bench warrant for Teal in his pocket,' the sheriff continued. 'It was Zee talked Mitch into tacking it to the cabin door at the Craven ranch.'

'Where did Mitch go when he rode away alone a while ago?' Pete asked the sheriff.

'Hard to tell. Mitch don't even say where he's bound for when he goes on one of his lone prowls. He's supposed to be under my orders, but he don't want any law officer to get mixed up in what he's doing. Mitch goes after one man at a time, crosses the man's name off his blacklist, then takes the trail of the next man he's going to kill. Nobody knows what kind of a deal he made with the Cattlemen's Association. Mitch Moran, killer, is a law unto himself, Pete.'

Pete Craven had to be content with that. He wanted to know the answers to a lot of questions that he dared not ask.

It was nearing sundown when Pete saddled two horses and took Nora for a ride. The sheriff had handed him a Winchester carbine, saying, 'Better take this along, Pete. And get back before dark.'

Pete had read the warning in the law officer's eyes as he shoved the carbine into his saddle scabbard and he and Nora rode into the sunset.

'I wish we could keep on going, Pete,' Nora said as they rode, stirrups touching. 'Mitch wants you to take me away before you get yourself killed. You're all I have left. Mom died in Denver and with Mitch dedicated to that job of his, life has nothing to hold for me. We're young, Pete, you and I. We're entitled to live our own lives. What is there to hold us here until you get shot down? You are no killer, Pete.'

'I know, Nora. But if I was to cut and run they'd follow until they caught up with me, like they did Mitch. You can't outrun a thing like that.'

'Mitch wrote on a pad that he'd cover our trail, kill anybody who tries to follow us. There's no cowardice in your running away, Pete. You owe nothing in the way of loyalty to Zee Dunbar. Let Mitch and Sheriff Ike Niber take care of Booger Red and the rest. Killing is a part of their job.'

'I've got to stay, Nora.'

'You think Mitch Moran was a stool-pigeon and a coward to run away, Pete. That's not true. Mitch turned informer in the hopes of saving Mom and me. Mitch never shot a man in his life until they cut him to pieces and left him to die in a snowdrift.' Nora's hand reached out to take Pete's hand in a firm grip. 'Let's keep on going now, Pete,' she pleaded.

'You don't understand,' Pete said. He was torn apart inside. Without turning his head to look at the girl, he told her about the little jockey, Stub Slade, and how he had to kill the pockmarked guard Nelson and Cottoneye Savage to avenge Stub's death.

'If your little friend could come back to life right now he would tell you to leave here and take me with you.' Nora's voice was vibrant. 'That would also be the advice of Deacon Arthur Jackson, who is your friend.'

'Where ... how ... when ...?' Pete's head twisted to look at her.

'Arthur and I are old friends. I used to meet every train at Chinook. I'd bring the porter a big lunch and he always had some little present for me. He never once let on that he got his meals free in the dining-car. On my way here a few days ago Arthur Jackson told me how he goes as often as he can to Slade Farm, and a lot about you, Pete.' Nora's fingers dug into Pete's hand. 'Arthur would tell you to get away from here. Tracy Dunbar told me to tell you to get away and take me with you, regardless of Zee Dunbar's hold on you.'

Pete Craven was about half convinced now that Nora was right. He lacked the killing instinct born into some men, acquired by others. If a man lacked that urge to kill it was apt to slow him up in the split-second timing that could mean the difference between life and death.

Before Pete could tell Nora how he felt the sharp crack of a carbine sounded somewhere in the gathering dusk. The harsh scream of mortal agony knifed through the gun echoes and became silent.

Pete leaned toward the girl and swept her off the saddle quickly, dropping to the ground with her. The Winchester carbine was gripped in his hand as they stood in the protective shelter of a high outbank. The two horses stood tracked in the high buckbrush that flanked the trail.

They waited, listening, narrowed eyes peering into the thickening shadows of night around them. Pete levered a cartridge from the box magazine into the breech and held the Winchester steady in a half-crouched position. Nora crouched beside him.

It seemed a long time before the sound of shod hoofs came. As the horsebacker came towards them, Pete motioned to Nora to crawl into the underbrush. He held the rider's shadowy figure in his gunsights as his horse came on at a slow jog-trot, the light too dim for recognition.

Pete felt Nora's nearness behind him, heard the sharp intake of her breath as she reached out and took hold of the carbine barrel, pulling it down.

'It's Mitch,' she whispered. 'Don't move till he's out of sight.' Nora moved close to him, shivering with a sudden chill. The blood had drained from her face and her eyes were dark and troubled.

They watched Mitch Moran ride past, his carbine barrel poised, ready to shoot at anything that moved or made a sound. For a brief moment the scarred face showed in the pale light of a rising moon under the low-pulled brim of his hat, white as a bleached skull, a distorted mask. A cold shudder wired Pete's spine as he watched horse and rider out of sight down the other side of the narrow hogback, Mitch looking back across his shoulder like a hunted animal.

'That's what's happened to my father,' Nora whispered, when the last sounds of the shod hoofs were no longer heard. 'That will happen to you, Pete, if you stay.'

Nora had no need to explain. Mitch Moran was no longer a human being with a man's normal reactions. He was like a maimed hydrophobic wolf on the prowl for his night victim. He had lost his birthright of civilized human rational actions and reactions, to pick up all the instincts of the hunted animal with a bounty on its pelt.

Sheriff Ike Niber had told Pete that Mitch was holed up at the old Kid Curry gang hide-away alone. Mitch would kill any man who had the damnfool temerity to ride down the steep slant to his cabin. The scars that made his face a hideous mask were nothing compared to the festering poisonous growth inside his heart and brain. His daughter Nora was the only person who had any control over Mitch, and hers was a slender thread that could snap and break at any instant.

Pete recalled the sheriff's grim words as he held Nora in his arms as she sobbed her tortured grief out, until it spent itself.

'You are all I have left, Pete,' Nora whispered. 'When I found out you'd been paroled and were at the Bradded Z Ranch, I quit my student nurse's training and rode the stage-coach to Malta. Sheriff Ike Niber arranged for me to come here with Steve Costello and Doctor Cole.' She gripped her hands tight around Pete's neck. 'Let's get away, Pete. Now. Before it's too late.'

There was a desperate appeal in her eyes that stripped away her courage and laid bare the woman's dread fear, revealing the stark terror she had lived with all these months.

'We'll go, Nora,' Pete told her.

The look in Nora's eyes had torn down his last barrier of what he had built up for his own man's courage during the long years. Pete owed nothing in the way of allegiance to Zee Dunbar and Nora had voiced his own desire to get away. It was what he had had in mind when he faced the parole board. Pete Craven had it made; until Steve Costello came up with his writ that put Pete into Zee Dunbar's so-called protective custody.

He wondered now what motive had prompted the attorney. There must be some deeply hidden motivation behind it. Surely Steve Costello held no love or loyalty for the crippled cowman.

Holding Nora in his arms, Pete stared out into the night with brooding eyes. As Nora lifted her head she caught the look of puzzlement in his scowl.

'To hell with Steve Costello and his shyster plans for his darling daughter!' Nora blurted out and pushed away. The brittle sound of her voice brought Pete back to reality.

'Daughter?' Pete said sharply. 'What are you talking about?' He flinched a little under the cold fury of her eyes.

'I'm talking about that chippy who married a man old enough to be her father. Zee Dunbar's wife, Tracy,' Nora's hands were clenched into tight fists. 'Damn her! Damn her! Damn her high-toned lady manner! That woman made love to you! Don't try to lie out of it!'

'I'm not trying to lie out of anything,' Pete said dully. He felt his face redden with remembered guilt.

'That lawyer of yours had you plead guilty, then had you paroled into Zee Dunbar's custody. He drew up Zee Dunbar's will that leaves everything to you, Pete, when he dies. He knew that if the crippled cowman didn't die of booze, somebody would shoot him. If Lance Rader didn't kill him, the job would fall to Pete Craven. Pete Craven, the sucker, who pleaded guilty of murder to save the soiled reputation of Tracy Dunbar.' Nora spat out the words.

'All you had to do was another killing job—Zee Dunbar. Steve Costello would get you off scot-free, so Pete Craven could marry Zee's widow, Steve Costello's long-lost daughter, and you'd own one of the biggest cow outfits in Montana.' Nora backed away from Pete, leaving him standing there in a sort of dazed bewilderment.

'Zee Dunbar had the will to live, so he made it,' Nora went on. 'He'll be back in circulation before long and nobody but him, and perhaps the devil in hell, knows what that tough cowman has in mind. He knows more than he lets on. Nobody has explained the shambles of the wrecked parlour. I'm damned if I'll ask any questions. I've talked too much as it is and I don't want answers to any questions.' The anger in Nora had burned itself out. It showed in her eyes as she came closer to Pete. 'Let's get away from the Bradded Z Ranch, Pete. That's all I ask of the man I love,' she pleaded softly.

'Nobody ever told me Tracy Dunbar was Steve Costello's daughter,' Pete said.

'Nobody knew it but Zee Dunbar and Steve Costello. Tracy herself doesn't know it, even now,' Nora explained.

'Then how come you know?' Pete asked.

'Zee Dunbar talked out of turn on the operating table. Doc Cole heard the story, too.'

'It's time we drifted out of here,' Pete said. He gave Nora a leg up and then swung into his saddle.

It was hard for Pete to believe that a man of Steve Costello's calibre would use him like that. Like Arthur Jackson, Pete had put the attorney on a high pedestal and not even Nora could drag the man down off it. He was too dazed and bewildered by the shock to try to puzzle it out. But there were too many facts and details bearing out the truth of Nora's angry outburst to push aside and toss into the discard.

No man likes to be used as Pete Craven felt

he had been used. Nora told the blunt truth when she called him a sucker. It was a hell of a jolt to a man's pride. The pride Pete had so slowly and laboriously built up from a quirted cowed kid.

Pete rode a little ahead of Nora, his saddle carbine in the crook of his left arm. When the dim twisting trail met the wagon road from the Bradded Z Ranch to the town of Landusky, they slowed down. Pete could see a branding corral in the moonlight a hundred yards away where the road crossed Rock Green. He reined up and motioned Nora to follow as he rode into a clump of high willows and dismounted.

'There's a saddled horse,' Pete whispered to Nora standing close beside him, 'near the corral, with the bridle off.' Pete pointed with the saddle carbine to the man hanging from a rope thrown over the cross-pole of the high gateway.

'That's where the sound of the shot came from. It looks like Mitch did a job on that one.' Pete handed the carbine to Nora. 'I have to find out who it is. You stay here.'

Pete mounted and loped off before Nora could voice a protest. He had a six-shooter in his hand as he rode up to the corral.

Pete had to look closely to recognize the hanged man. Mitch had cut and slashed at the face until it was a blood-smeared mask. But when the pallid skin was free from drying blood, the pitted pockmarks showed like dark purple indentations. There was no doubt in Pete's mind that the hanged man was the pockmarked Nelson.

Pete rode up to the saddled horse and dropped his catch rope over its head and led the animal back to where Nora was waiting.

'It was the reform school guard, Nelson,' Pete told her as he swung to the ground.

He unsaddled the horse. There was a 30-30 Winchester carbine in the saddle scabbard and a small muslin salt sack filled with cartridges tied to the saddle strings of the new-looking saddle.

'The way I read the sign,' Pete said, 'Nelson had been waiting there for some time. A few live coals were in the supper fire and coffee still warm in the lard pail he used for a coffee-pot. He'd laid out part of a slab of bacon on a board and opened a can of baked beans and tomatoes. Mitch shot him while he was getting his supper ready, then cut his face to ribbons and strung him up.

'I think Nelson was contact man for the Cattle Rustlers' Syndicate. I reckon he was waiting for Teal to show up with the money Zee Dunbar was to pay for the drive of stolen cattle Booger Red is bringing from Wyoming.'

'Let's get away,' Nora whispered. She pointed to two horsebackers along the moonlit skyline.

'Too late for a getaway now. They'd sight us.' Pete's voice was grimly quiet. 'We'll bush up a ways down the creek from this crossing. We'll take to the creek. Water leaves no horse tracks.'

They left Nelson's horse grazing along the bank and rode downstream. The water was stirrup high and Pete and Nora had to bend low over the saddle horns to keep from being scraped off by the low-hanging brush along both sides of the narrow creek. It was like riding through a dark tunnel of some underground stream.

When the brush closed in ahead, they reined up to listen to the voices at the corral behind them, simplified in the night's silence.

'What the hell!' A man's voice sounded, saw-edged with alarm. 'Looky yonder, Teal!'

'Get an eyeful, Purty Boy. If you ain't never seen a hanged man before, you're lookin' at one now.'

'Who is it, Teal?'

'Why don't you lope over and see for yourself, Rader,' Teal said. Then added, 'I can tell from here it's that pockmarked bastard, Nelson. He was waiting here for the payoff.'

'Mitch Moran's trademark,' Rader said harshly. 'Face cut to ribbons, maybe the tongue cut out. I'm gettin' to hell away!'

'If you need a brave maker, Rader, look around for Nelson's jug. He ain't got it in his hand, that's for sure,' Teal said.

Lance Rader reined his horse and started back along the trail they had used to reach the corral.

'Where the hell do you think you're headed for?' called Teal, a menacing chuckle undertoning his words.

'Back to the Craven place. With Mitch Moran on the prowl, you're not sucking me into a gun trap at the Bradded Z Ranch. I don't like the look of things, Teal.'

Pete could see Teal as he rode over to block the range dude's trail.

'Get a tailholt of yourself, Purty Boy.' Teal's voice was as coldly threatening as the carbine he shoved into Lance Rader's ribs. 'Nobody's shoving you into any gun trap. You're a valuable piece of property to Teal; my ace in the hole. You're marryin' Zee Dunbar's widder. Remember?' Teal's gun prodded him.

'Zee ain't dead yet,' Lance Rader's voice was thin.

'You had it set up for you at Butte,' Teal said. 'You made a mess of it. Now it's my turn. I'll guarantee results.'

'Then have at it,' Lance Rader said. 'Deal me out of the game.'

'I said you were my hole card. Zee wants to see you. I told him I'd bring you. Teal's a man of his word, Purty Boy.'

'You'd like to get me killed. You're a cold-blooded son of a bitch, Teal,' Lance Rader shrilled.

'We had the same bitch for a mother,' Teal said. 'But not the same father. There's a hell of a difference, Purty Boy. My old man was tough as a boot. Yours was a tinhorn sport.'

'You shot my father in the back. Murdered him in cold blood. I saw you do it,' Rader said.

'Yeah. I can be picked up on that bench warrant for the murder of a saloon owner and gambler named Blackjack Rader. But if ever I come up for trial, you'll swear under oath that I shot in self-defence, Purty Boy.'

'Like hell I will, Teal.'

'The hell you won't,' Teal said flatly. 'I'm killin' Zee Dunbar before he gets a shot at you. When you marry Zee's widder I get my cut. With Booger Red ramroddin' the Cattle Rustlers' Syndicate and supplyin' the Bradded Z with stolen cattle, we can't lose. We got the world by the tail, Purty Boy.'

'I don't like it. No matter what kind of a big

set-up you're buildin' up.'

'I kill Zee Dunbar,' Teal went on. 'You take Booger Red's whelp outa circulation. It's like shootin' fish in a rain barrel. We can't lose.'

'You can't sluff Mitch Moran into the discard,' Lance Rader said.

'We'll sucker that gun-locoed bastard into a gun trap and put an end to his misery. I got it all figgered out. One of these nights he'll ride down the slant to the Hideaway and we'll be waitin'.' Teal reined away, motioning Lance Rader to follow him. He rode over to the dead camp fire and leaning down from the saddle he hooked a finger through the handle of a brown jug.

'What you need is a few swallows of rotgut to warm the fear in your guts, Purty Boy.' Teal shoved the jug at Rader.

Pete relaxed his tension on the carbine, lowering it as they watched Teal and Lance Rader ride away into the rough breaks and out of sight.

'I can't run out now, Nora,' Pete said quietly. 'We're headin' back for the Bradded Z Ranch.'

'Why?' Nora said in a dead tone.

'I got to live with myself,' Pete said. 'I couldn't look into my eyes in a shavin' mirror.'

'And I don't like beards.' Nora's lips forced a smile that left her eyes dark with dread. When Pete kissed her he felt the cold stiffness of her lips.

When it was safe to leave, they mounted and Pete led the way back through the dark tunnel of overhanging brush to the gravel crossing.

With Teal and Lance Rader headed for the Bradded Z Ranch and the gun-crazy Mitch Moran on the prowl, it made the way back dangerous. The safest bet was to hole up somewhere until daylight and Pete remembered a line camp a few miles away.

'We'll stay at the Squaw Butte line camp tonight,' he told Nora. 'Like as not there'll be a hay crew camped there. Anyhow there'll be grub and I could do with a big pot of black round-up coffee.'

'With whiskers on it,' Nora said. 'I'm the gal can make it.'

CHAPTER FOURTEEN

There was the clean fresh smell of new-mown hay as Pete and Nora rode up to the Squaw Butte Line Camp. There was no sign of human life. The door of the log cabin was closed. Pete made Nora stay behind as he prowled the barn and cabin. He waved from the cabin doorway for her to come on. He lit a candle in the neck of a whisky bottle and started the fire in the small sheet iron camp stove.

While Nora made the coffee, he unsaddled the horses and after watering them, he put them in the barn, forking hay into the mangers and bedding the stalls, then went to the cabin.

He nailed an old blanket across the window and barred the door from the inside. The coffee was simmering on the back of the stove, the bacon fried and a skillet of raw potatoes frying and a pan of biscuits in the oven.

Nora had her sleeves rolled up above the elbows and a clean flour-sack apron tied around her slim waist. Her face was flushed as she poured steaming black coffee into two tin cups. She put the pot back on the stove and turned around slowly. There was a tremulous smile on her red lips as she met the look in Pete's eyes and walked across the room into his outstretched arms. This was the first time they had ever been actually alone together and they both were keenly aware of it.

The coffee grew cold in the tin cups. The fire in the camp stove burned to ashes. The pan of biscuits stayed in the oven and the bacon and potatoes congealed in the cooling bacon grease. The stub of candle melted down and the flame flickered out, leaving the cabin in darkness.

Man being a creature of habit, Pete came awake when the dawn of a new day greyed the blanket across the window. He had the blanket pulled aside and was peering out the window, a carbine in his hand, when he heard Nora whisper from the dark shadows, 'What is it, Pete?' Fear sharpened the words as she came to the window to look out.

Pete pointed towards the horsebacker who was just riding out of sight. It was Mitch Moran. When he had gone Pete unbarred the door and went to the barn.

He came back a little while later with a sheet of paper with pencilled writing on it. He told Nora he had found it tacked to the barn door. He handed it to her and she read:

'*This won't make you bullet-proof, Pete. But it gives you a hunting licence to kill anything that gets in your way. Pin it on the outside of your shirt where it will show.*' It was signed Mitch.

Pete showed Nora the small nickel-plated shield with the words 'Livestock Inspector' stamped in the metal.

'The law badge was hung on a nail beside the note. It's the one he's been wearing pinned to his undershirt. Looks like he followed us here,' Pete said. 'Mitch could have stayed for breakfast, anyhow.'

'Mitch is sensitive about his scarred face. He has a little trouble eating so he goes off alone.' Nora took the badge and pinned it to the pocket of Pete's blue flannel shirt.

'I'll do the barn chores while you get breakfast.' Pete smiled faintly. 'I reckon Mitch Moran is going to ride close herd on us from now on.' He kissed her and went out.

A strange silence fell like a pall during breakfast. Once or twice they attempted a forced gaiety that fell flat, tasteless as the warmed-over bacon and biscuits. This was the tomorrow that had come for them, with its invisible cloud of threatening danger that Pete had chosen to face. The summer sun was an hour high in the cloudless blue of the Montana sky when Pete Craven and Nora Moran rode up to the Bradded Z Ranch.

Steve Costello and Doctor Cole sat smoking in silence on the broad veranda, their armchairs tilted back, their feet on the railing, looking out across the country beyond.

Save for these two, the ranch had a deserted look. Doctor Cole waved a stilted greeting as Pete and Nora reined up at the long hitch-rack.

Pete swung to the ground and came up the steps. Nora sat stiffly in her saddle.

Pete paused uncertainly as he stood on the porch, eyeing the pair of strangely silent men.

'Sheriff Ike Niber,' Doctor Cole answered the question in Pete's eyes, 'pulled out before daybreak, a little while after Mitch Moran rode up. Ike called for volunteers and every cowpuncher, including the cook, went along, like a cow outfit starting out on a round-up. Zee Dunbar slipped out of the house, saddled up and was gone before daybreak.'

'Did the sheriff leave any message for me?' Pete asked uneasily.

'Not that I know of.'

'Zee?' Pete's throat was dry. 'I'm farmed out to Zee Dunbar.'

Steve Costello took a long brown manila envelope from the inside pocket of his corduroy jacket and tossed it towards Pete, who caught it.

'That's the Governor's pardon restoring the citizenship of Pete Craven,' the attorney said. 'You are no longer in bondage to any man, save yourself.'

Steve Costello slid his booted feet from the railing. He got up from his chair and walked into the house. There was an empty whisky bottle alongside the vacant chair that Pete had not noticed before.

'Tracy Dunbar is dead. Shot herself last night,' Doctor Cole said. 'Steve is taking it hard.'

Pete went down the steps to the hitchrack. Helping Nora dismount he told her what had happened. His arm was across her shoulders as they went back up the steps. Pete pulled up two chairs for Nora and himself near where the doctor sat in brooding silence.

'I'd left a sedative for Tracy to take but she didn't take it,' Doctor Cole said. 'She must have sat up alone most of the night. Steve and I slept together in Zee's big brass bed upstairs, but sometime long after midnight I came awake suddenly and found that Steve wasn't sharing the bed with me. There was a strange sort of echo in the room but it was gone before I could identify it.

'The sheriff had left before we went to bed. He was worried about you two when you didn't come back, so he saddled up and I took some of the cowpunchers along to search for you. I thought perhaps it was the returning posse that woke me, but the bunkhouse was in darkness and all was quiet outside.

'I dressed and went downstairs. The door of the smoking-room stood ajar and in the dim lamplight I saw Steve stretched out face down on the couch, his head hidden in his arms, dry sobs tearing him apart.

'I crept back upstairs to Zee's bedroom and closed the door. I pulled up a chair to the window and with a bottle of Zee's whisky, I sat there until the break of day when I saw the sheriff and his posse ride in. Then I went back downstairs.

'Steve Costello was standing at the foot of the stairs, his face like a death mask. "Tracy killed herself, Doc," he said. "Tracy's dead and there's nothing you can do."

'I told him I was bound by law as a doctor to examine the body. Steve motioned towards the smoking-room. I found Tracy dead in a chair in the corner of the room, the gun on the floor where it had dropped from her hand.' Doctor Cole reached for his hip flask and unscrewed the metal cap.

Pete and Nora watched as he gulped down the raw whisky until the flask was drained. Then Pete got slowly to his feet, saying, 'I'm going in there.' He dropped the long brown envelope in Nora's lap. 'Alone,' he added, as he crossed the porch and opened the front door, closing it behind him.

Pete found Steve Costello sitting in a big horsechair-cushioned chair in the front parlour. He was bent over, long legs spread out, holding a whisky bottle in both hands. His head lifted and Pete saw the terrible stricken look in the man's sunken eyes.

Pete longed to tell the man that he wanted to share whatever he had for a burden of grief.

He recalled the Negro porter's words ... 'Cap'n Steve helps others ... won't let nobody help him ...' But Pete was too clumsy with words to risk saying so. He pulled up a chair and sat down beside the stricken man.

'Tracy was my daughter,' Steve Costello said as he looked at Pete with burned-out eyes. 'She was only three years old when my wife took her and ran away with another man. Just out of law school I'd married an actress who was beautiful as sin, but vindictive. She never wanted a baby and because I worshipped the child she ran off with a gambler and took Tracy from me.

'The train they left on was wrecked. My wife and baby were on the list of dead, while the gambler escaped with slight injuries. I followed his trail and shot him down in San Francisco where I found him. I defended myself in court, pleaded the Unwritten Law, and was acquitted.

'I had no way of knowing the blackguard had persuaded my faithless wife to leave the baby at an orphanage. I had given him no chance to talk when I shot him down. Sixteen years later, Zee Dunbar married a young girl from the dance halls. Zee had been on one of his drunks and had shot and killed two men in a drunken brawl. He sent for me to defend him. Zee was guilty as hell and I told him so, refusing to take his case. He said he'd killed the men for making insulting remarks about his young wife, and I told him that was to be expected when he married a girl from the dance halls. He laughed in my face and told me that the girl he married was my own daughter, Tracy, who had run away from an orphanage. He threatened to smear her name over the State of Montana.

'I cleared Zee Dunbar of the double charge of murder. It took every trick I knew. I blackened the names of the two murdered men in court. I used Zee Dunbar's money to bribe eyewitnesses who were not there. It was as disgracefully shameful as it was brilliant and clever. I should have been disbarred from the Montana law courts. It was my last case until I defended you and the reputation of the same lady.' He smiled bitterly as he drank from the bottle.

'Tracy was unaware of her true parentage. That was a part of the agreement I made with Zee Dunbar. Zee had somehow found Tracy's birth record. He had the birth certificate locked in his safe. Last night he unlocked the safe to get what money was there and left it open. Tracy found her birth certificate after Zee had saddled up and left before daylight. She must have felt a great bitterness towards the world and me.

'When I heard the shot I ran downstairs and found her dead.'

Steve Costello got up and paced the floor for a long while before he halted within a few feet of Pete. His voice sounded husky when he spoke. 'I wanted you, Pete, to marry Tracy in case Zee was killed. You were somewhat in love with Tracy then, fighting it back because she was the wife of Zee Dunbar. I had grown to like you, Pete, because you were clean and decent and had the makings of a man. I was trying to play God in uniting the two persons who were already close together in my heart.' Steve turned away abruptly and crossed the room to stare out the window. 'Perhaps this will explain why I had you paroled to Zee Dunbar, Pete. I wanted you and Tracy to fall in love. I'd hoped the liquor Zee was drinking and the injury to his spine would cause his death before long. I already had Zee draw up his will leaving the Bradded Z to you, Pete.'

'I understand, Steve.' Pete walked to the window and laid his hand on the man's shoulder. 'But too much had already happened to stack the odds against Tracy and me. Tracy must have known that.'

'Yes, Tracy knew. I wanted too long to tell her the truth and my plans for her. She had fallen deeply in love with you, Pete, but there was Nora. The gun was handy and she took the easiest way out.'

CHAPTER FIFTEEN

The sun was still high when a horsebacker came into sight. It was Zee Dunbar and he was leading a horse with the body of a dead man roped across the blood-caked saddle.

Pete got up from his chair on the porch where he and Steve Costello had been sitting for some time. He was at the hitchrack when Zee reined up.

The cowman sat squarely in his saddle, leaning a little forward across the horn. His face with its stubble of grey whiskers was gaunt and lined with fatigue, his eyes bloodshot slivers of pale light under the slanted brim of his old sweat-marked hat. He stank sourly of booze and sweat, and his hands gripping the saddle horn were dirty, crusted with dried blood.

'I fetched back Lance Rader,' Zee Dunbar's voice came from behind bared clenched teeth, 'for my wife to look at. Lance ain't purty any more. Get your rump outa that chair, Steve, and bring Tracy out here. I want her to see what's left of her fancy man.'

Steve Costello sat in his chair, silently staring at the cowman.

'Tracy!' Zee lifted his voice to a harsh bellow. 'Tracy! You got special company! Get out here!'

The blood came back into the cowman's face as the dull echoes of his own shouted words came back to mock him.

'Your wife's dead,' Steve Costello said coldly. 'Tracy shot herself. You've hurt her for the last time, you sadistic son of a bitch.'

Zee Dunbar saw the look in Steve Costello's eyes as the grim truth of his words seeped into his exhausted, whisky-fumed brain. He scowled a little but said nothing as he slid the lead rope from his saddle horn, letting it drop to the ground.

Pete felt the brutal force of the cowman's stare as it probed him.

'Me'n Mitch Moran set a gun trap,' Zee said. 'Mitch has Teal on ice at the Craven place. Booger Red's comin' into the trap when he crosses his herd of stolen cattle tomorrow mornin'. You got Mitch's tin badge pinned to your shirt. You goin' to play your tough hand, Pete?' Zee spat out the words.

'You don't need to take orders,' Steve Costello said loudly, 'from Zee Dunbar or any man, Pete.'

'I know, Steve,' Pete said quietly, never

taking his eyes from Zee's bloodshot stare. 'But I'm playin' my hand out. I want to be on hand when Booger Red and Cottoneye Savage cross their cattle.'

Zee Dunbar grinned wolfishly as he reined his horse and headed back, leaving the horse with its grisly burden standing tracked at the hitchrack.

'Keep Nora in the house, Steve,' Pete said as he picked up the hackamore rope. 'Tell her I'll look after myself.'

Pete led the horse to the barn. He told one of the cowhands to get the pack off and turn the horse loose. One glance at the dead man was enough for Pete. It looked as if Zee Dunbar had stood back a ways and emptied his six-shooter into Lance Rader's face.

Pete saddled and shoved his carbine into the saddle scabbard. As he rode off he saw Nora in the porch waving. He waved his hat as he lifted his horse to a lope.

When he overtook the cowman, they rode along in a heavy silence. Zee had a fat brown jug hung to the horn of his saddle by a whang leather loop. He kept drinking from it as they rode along. Pete hoped he wouldn't start asking questions about Tracy because he had no answers to give.

'I got rid of Sheriff Ike Niber,' Zee finally said, staring ahead with a fixed gaze. 'Sent him back to Chinook. I don't want no damned law man underfoot when we spring the trap on the Cattle Rustlers' Syndicate. That tin badge you're wearing is all that's needed. I hope I'm there to see the look on Booger Red's face when he sees a law badge pinned on you. I hope you got the guts to shine it in his eyes.'

Pete was riding on his right. As he watched Zee drink, his hand closed around the butt of his own gun. If the cowman was working himself up to one of his treacherous gun plays, Pete made up his mind to beat him to it.

'You ever figure out,' Zee's hand came away from his gun as his eyes swivelled to look sideways at Pete, 'why I sent that drunken bulldozer Jim West to serve that bench warrant on you?'

'I think I know by this time,' Pete answered, watching the cowman narrowly.

'I caught Tracy makin' eyes at you but I never let on,' Zee said. 'I was scared to come back that night for fear I'd find what Jim West found when he broke down the door. I'm a tough son of a bitch and I've been provin' it all along. But I didn't have the guts to find out the truth. Because I loved my wife.' Zee's face twitched. 'Steve Costello called me sadistic and that's the size of it. Tracy gave me a reason.'

Zee's eyes narrowed when he said, 'Steve

Costello has good reasons for hating my guts. So have you, kid.' He grinned. 'You hate my damned guts, Pete?' he asked.

'No,' Pete said quietly. 'I don't hate you, Zee. You've been giving yourself more punishment than ever you dealt out. You're living in hell right now.'

'I don't want any man's pity,' Zee said harshly. 'I don't want no man feelin' sorry for Zee Dunbar.' The sweat broke out on the cowman's face and he gripped the saddle horn with both blood-crusted hands to keep from falling off. That thirty-mile ride was the longest Pete had ever remembered.

The sun was sinking behind the broken skyline of the badlands when Pete and Zee rode down the long scrub-pine-spotted ridge to the Craven place.

Strange emotions filled Pete as he sighted the pole corrals, the long cattle shed and barn, the log cabin on the banks of the big Missouri River. This was the place where Pete Craven had spent the long years of his boyhood that held all its bitter memories that came crowding back now. Cold sweat broke out under his eyes at the thought of facing Booger Red in all his cold fury as he pictured it; the look in the bloodshot green eyes; the contemptuous sneer on the red-bearded lips.

Pete didn't know for sure if his boyhood

fear was still deep inside him but he hoped that when the showdown came he'd have the guts to face it like a man.

When they rode up to the cabin Pete helped the cowman from the saddle and held him upright on weakened legs. The cabin door opened and Teal stood framed in the doorway, a bandage around his head, his face masked with pain. Both arms were raised to the level of his shoulders, both hands wrapped in bloodstained bandages.

'Mitch creased Teal's head with a 30–40 steel-jacket bullet that knocked him loose from his saddle while I was shooting at Lance Rader,' Zee explained to Pete. 'While Teal was out like a light Mitch cut the leaders in both hands. If he lives that long his fingers will cramp and shrivel up like dead bird claws.'

Zee unbuckled the strap of one of his saddle pockets. He took out a bulging canvas sack. He tossed the sack and it landed in the dirt at Teal's feet.

'You kept your word about bringing Lance Rader to the Bradded Z Ranch, Teal,' Zee Dunbar said. 'I told you I was willing to pay for it. All the money that was in the safe is in that sack. That pays you off, Teal. I kept my end of the bargain.'

Teal's lipless mouth twisted in a sardonic

grin as he looked at the bloodstained bandages covering the mutilated hands that would never again riffle a deck of cards or grip the butt of a six-shooter.

His cartridge belt, every loop filled with brass shells, sagged slanted across his lean flanks, but the holster tied down on his thigh held no gun.

Even so the killer from the Wyoming cattle war had a menacing look as he stood in the cabin doorway. Teal would always be dangerous as long as there was life in him.

The sound of a shot came from across the river, a second shot picking up its echo, then a third shot that left a tense silence in the sunset.

'That will be Booger Red,' Teal said, 'come for his South America stake.'

'There's enough in that sack,' Zee grinned crookedly, 'to buy you and him both a one-way ticket to hell.' He motioned with his gun barrel to the bulging sack. 'Pick up your taw, Teal.'

Teal picked up the sack with his bandaged hands and shoved it inside the sweat-sodden blood-spotted black sateen shirt.

'You made your dicker with the Cattle Rustlers' Syndicate, Teal,' Zee said coldly. 'Take my horse and ride out on the sandbar. Tell Booger Red to hit the river with the cattle; that you got the pay-off money.'

Teal walked over to where Zee's horse was standing. He locked both wrists across the saddle horn and mounted, and rode out on a wide strip of sand, reining up at the water's edge.

A moment later a horsebacker on the far bank rode out of the brush. 'That you, Teal?' bellowed a harsh saw-edged voice.

A thin shiver ran down Pete Craven's spine as he heard the sound of Booger Red's rasping voice.

'It's me, Booger Red!' said Teal.

'You got it?'

'I got better than top market price. Cross your herd and pick up the marbles.'

'I'll cross the cattle directly the sun gets off the river. Cattle don't take to swimming water with the sun blindin' their eyes. By the time the leaders get here the sun should be off the water. The boys might run into a little hell holdin' 'em up to fan 'em out. I come a long ways with this cattle drive and I don't aim to pile 'em up at no river crossin'.'

The wide Missouri caught the last slanted rays of the sun before it went down behind the broken badlands skyline. The sounds of bawling thirsty cattle came across the river and the strung-out cattle drive came into sight on the bald hogback ridge that was sparsely spotted with scrub pines. With the drab clay ridge turned Indian red in the sunset glow, the long horns picked up the reflected colour and tossed it back. Two cowhands rode the point as the lead steers came down the slope, then the swing riders came into view out of the red dust kicked up by the shuffling cloven hoofs.

The sounds of the bawling cattle, the click of cloven hoofs, the thud of horses' feet, the jingle of spurs and bit chains, the creak of saddle leather and a cowboy's plaintive song blended into fitting orchestration.

It pinched the heart of young Pete Craven as he viewed it with an inward look that touched something deep inside his being, stirring a nostalgia there he had never known existed. This was his home, this was his life, and he was a part of it. The roots of boyhood were here on the banks of the Missouri. The song of the river came to him, seeping into him, filling his heart that had been emptied, melting the bitterness and heartaches. Pete Craven knew that if God let him live he would stay here forever.

Something of the feeling that stirred young Pete must have touched the grizzled cowman. 'You'll never see the like to that again,' Zee Dunbar spoke in a hushed tone, as if he were giving voice to his innermost thoughts.

The cowman's words aroused Pete from his

own musings. Red and his horse were no longer in sight. Teal was riding back, letting the horse pick its own shuffling running walk.

The sun had gone down and the river looked grey. The broken badlands beyond had taken on a forbidding shadow and out of that darkened maw the cattle were spewing. The cowboys on the point and those on the swing had ridden out ahead. A dozen cowhands were riding back and forth, yelling, slapping rawhide quirts and doubled ropes to spread out the bawling trotting steers, to let the lead cattle drink their fill and move out across the river before those behind rode them down in their crazed thirst.

'Spread 'em out!' Booger Red's shout rode over the din. 'Fan 'em out!' He spurred his horse along the solid front of cattle, cursing any cowpuncher who wasn't making a hand.

Booger Red and half a dozen cowhands rode out ahead of the lead steers that drank and waded into the water, prodded by the horns in their giant rumps.

The quarter-mile strip of river was packed with thirsty cattle that hooked and bawled, walleyed, stringing threads of slobber. A cowpuncher had to know his job, have the cow savvy and cool-headed guts to know when to give way, when to ride into the water to save yourself and the horse he rode from being caught and hooked down and trampled to death.

Booger Red cursed his renegade cowhands, keeping them there when every man wanted to ride into the swimming water, out of the wide path of danger. The half-dozen men with Booger Red were thinking to hell with the damned cattle, let 'em pile up and be trampled into a bawling crippled mass. A man's life was worth more than all the stolen cattle that ever came out of Wyoming to each of that tough crew of cowhands. But not to Booger Red's way of thinking. These two-bit renegades were a dime a dozen. Kill 'em all and you wouldn't get a real man among 'em.

'Stand your ground, you yellow-bellied sons a hell!' Booger Red's ugly bellow sounded. 'Earn that easy money you've been gettin'. Hold these cattle, fan 'em out!'

Pete had never seen Cottoneye Savage on horseback, but he could see the hulking towhead now at the far end of the lead cattle. Even at the distance across the river there was no mistaking him. He wore a bright red flannel shirt and a ten gallon high-crowned, wide-brimmed hat and a pair of white angora wool chaps. Pete knew that once the hair of the chaps got wet, together with the weight of a filled cartridge belt and six-shooter and his two-hundred-pound bulk that sat the silver mounted saddle like a sack of wet bran, there would be too much dead weight for the horse he rode to carry, if he hit swimming water.

Cottoneye was dressed like one of the dude cowboys from Buffalo Bill's Wild West Show, even to the pinto horse. Right now he was worse than useless as he spurred down through the shallow water, panicked by fear of the solid block of moving cattle that were almost on top of him and his pinto horse.

At the lower end of the crossing was an almost perpendicular clay bank, choked with willow brush on top. There was a beaver slide, wet and slippery, as if it had been smeared with axle grease, that cut into the bank where the water was ten feet deep. It had the deceptive appearance of a wide cattle trail and Cottoneye was headed for that as a means of escaping the onrush of cattle.

Two or three cowpunchers shouted warnings as Cottoneye spurred past. They were hollering at him to pull up. To shed his wool chaps before he took to the river. To give his horse its head and the pinto would swim across.

'I ain't goin' across!' Cottoneye's voice was shrill with terror. 'I'm goin' ashore here and back to the drags where I belong! That Booger Red had no business gettin' me into it. He knows I can't swim a lick!'

'That's swimmin' water you're ridin' into, you damn fool mail-order cowboy,' a cowpuncher shouted after him as he neared the clay bank.

The big pinto's forelegs stepped into a deep water-hole that somersaulted the animal. Cottoneye was thrown clear as the horse went under the surface.

Pete stared out at the red shirt and its flailing arms, the legs encased in the white angora chaps spread awkwardly as the two-hundred-pound Cottoneye landed in a sprawled-out belly flop. His terrified scream knifed through the din of bawling cattle, the clash of horns, then was blotted out as his head went under water. The ten gallon hat floated on the water.

Booger Red had spurred after him, cursing him. He had a loop swinging in his rawhide reata as Cottoneye's tow-head surfaced. The loop shot out on a thirty-foot length of rawhide rope, dropping over the sodden head. Booger Red jerked the slack as the noose came down around the thick neck. He had Cottoneye head-roped and as his flailing arms and shoulders came above the surface, Booger Red shouted at him, 'Grab the rope, you drowned useless bastard! You're holdin' up the outfit!'

It is doubtful if the half-drowned, terrified

Cottoneye heard. The hands that gripped the wet slippery plaited raw-hide reata were the desperate reflex of a drowning man.

His horse was stirrup deep in water when Booger Red reined him around and dragged Cottoneye from the deep water on to a narrow strip of sandbar. His stained teeth bared in a whiskered grin as he took the winds from his saddle horn and shook slack in the wet rope, then called to the nearest rider to get down and take off his ketch rope.

The black and white pinto had surfaced and was fifty yards down stream swimming for shore.

The cowhand leaned from his saddle to free the noose from around Cottoneye's neck. He straightened in the saddle as he tossed the end with the heavy hondo back towards the red-whiskered ramrod.

'You got the job done, Booger Red,' he called. 'That big tough meat Cottoneye was always braggin' about pulled his spine apart at the last joint. You broke his neck when you dragged him ashore. The one-eyed kid was due to stretch rope anyhow. Maybe Long Tom Savage will whittle you out a leather medal, Booger Red, when he gets here with the drags.'

'Keep them cattle comin', and keep that damned waggin' tongue of yours behind your teeth!' Booger Red snarled as he turned his horse and swam across the river ahead of the swimming cattle.

Pete Craven and Zee Dunbar sat their horses in the darkened shadow of the big pole corral. Teal had gotten his own horse from the barn and was riding out at a slow walk to meet Booger Red.

The big red-whiskered ramrod of the Cattle Rustlers' Syndicate had come ashore on the sandbar as the lead steers splashed wearily through the shallow water. As he lifted each leg to let the water run from his boot-tops he barked out orders to the half-dozen cowhands who kept the cattle moving, to scatter out to graze as they came ashore. On the far bank Long Tom Savage and the rest of the cowboys were shoving the drag end of the herd into the river.

Pete had witnessed the death of Cottoneye Savage. With Nelson dead, the debt of little Stub Slade had been paid off in full. Each had met the violent end they deserved. Pete had taken no part in either death and he was duly thankful.

'Spit on that tin badge,' Zee said in a lowered tone. 'Polish 'er up. Shine it into Booger Red's mean eyes and maybe it'll blind him so's you can get in the first shot at the bushwhacker who killed your father and laid claim to his widow.'

It took a long moment for the meaning of the cowman's words to register in Pete's brain.

'Booger Red Craven,' Pete said, his voice sharp with suspicion of the treacherous, half-drunken cowman, 'is the only father I ever knew.'

'Didn't Mitch Moran show you the name scratched on that stock inspector's badge you're wearin'?' Zee asked.

'No,' Pete said.

'Maybe Mitch forgot on purpose. Mitch Moran was there when Booger Red set the gun trap for Pete Walters, the stock inspector who was cold trailin' him with a bunch of stolen horses. Pete Walters was murdered and his carcass weighted down with an old mowin' machine wheel and sunk in the river. A month later Booger Red showed his law badge to his widow at her millinery shop in Chinook. He told her some kind of a lie about Pete Walters having quit the country and sent her the badge as proof. Booger Red talked her into getting a divorce and selling the hat shop. They were married but in a few months she gave birth to Pete Walters's baby boy. Mitch Moran's wife raised you when your mother died in childbirth. When you were too young to remember Booger Red claimed you. He'd really loved your mother and blamed you for her death.

'I got the story from Mitch a few days before you were paroled to me. He put it in writing and his wife signed it with him. It's locked in my safe.' Zee drank from his jug and rammed the cork down with the heel of his hand, hanging the jug from his saddle horn.

'You're the spittin' image of Stock Inspector Pete Walters about the time Booger Red shot him in the back.' A crafty grin spread the grey stubbled face. 'Shine your real daddy's law badge in his face and see what happens, Pete Walters.'

There was no doubting the truth of the cowman's words. Little things, half-forgotten, half-remembered, came back into Pete's memory like long scattered bits of a jigsaw puzzle, dropping into place. The name of Pete Walters was the key to the solving of the puzzle. Wild Pete Walters had ridden the rough string for every big outfit in Montana. Wild, reckless, without a taint of cowardice in his make-up, Pete Walters had left his mark as a top cowhand and later as a stock inspector.

A warm glow filled the empty coldness inside Pete as he fingered the nickel-plated law badge. There was not a drop of Booger Red Craven's blood in his veins, and it was as if a doctor had given him a blood test for some loathsome disease and told him his blood was clean.

He was the son of the almost legendary Pete Walters. It was something to be proud about. He understood now the full meaning of why Mitch Moran had given him the law badge.

Mitch would be hushed up right now somewhere within gunshot range to back his play when the chips were down. This was the final showdown. Mitch Moran had waited until the son of the murdered Pete Walters had grown to manhood and could take his own part before he had checked the bet to him.

Booger Red Craven, standing high in his long stirrups, twisted around and waved his hat at a tall gaunt-looking raw-boned man who was riding ashore on the sandbar.

'Come and git it, Savage! Teal's wearin' white mittens like ol' Zee Dunbar's money was too hot to handle bare-handed. Tell them tough hands to keep their heads up. I can smell a guntrap.' There was a long-barrelled Colt six-shooter in Booger Red's hand when he rode up to where Teal sat his horse.

'If it's a bushwhacker trap,' the gun gripped in the big red hair tufted hand pointed at Teal's belly, 'you'll be the first to get a dose of lead poison, Teal.'

Teal's black Stetson rode at a low-pulled slant across his bandaged head. The beady black eyes bored into the red-whiskered face. There was bitter contempt in Teal's lipless grin. 'Move slow and speak easy, Booger Red. Your old side partner, Mitch Moran, is bushed up somewheres nearby.'

Booger Red's whiskered grin twisted into a snarl as he crowded his horse into Teal's. 'You double-crosser, Teal. What the hell goes on here?'

'Hard to tell till the chips are down,' Teal said calmly. 'Zee tied the can to my bushy tail. He's here himself to tally out the cattle in your Question Mark road iron. I got the money on me. Zee filled Lance Rader full of lead. Mitch Moran gutshot Nelson and then hung him. He creased my head with a bullet and knocked me out of the saddle, then cut the leaders in both of my hands. That's how come I got 'em wrapped up. I can't hold a gun or pull a trigger. Zee sent me out to close the deal on the wet cattle.'

'This has the earmarks of a guntrap, Teal!' snarled Booger Red.

Teal grinned flatly, then said, 'Mitch Moran pinned Pete Walters' stock inspector badge on his son, the boy you quirted around since he was a button of a kid. Young Pete Walters is holdin' your herd up for a law cut. Looks like he's playing his murdered father's hand out.'

Every nerve in Pete's body was wire tight, every muscle tense, and there was a cold deadly co-ordination between mind and body that made for the split-second timing of the six-shooter gripped in his hand as he gave his horse its head. The horse, as if sensing the tautness of the rider, travelled at a steady walk.

Pete could make out the hard cold glint of Booger Red's slivered bloodshot eyes, green as the eyes of a coiled rattler. Those were the same eyes that had put the chill of fear into his kid's guts. He was no longer afraid of the big red-whiskered man as his cold grey eyes met the deadly threat there. His gun was held in a steady grip. There was nothing of a braggart's gesture as his left hand brushed over the badge pinned to his shirt.

Teal backed his horse slowly away out of the line of gunfire.

'That pinto came ashore without Cottoneye!' the harsh rasping voice of Long Tom Savage called out. 'What happened to that kid of mine, Booger Red?'

Pete saw the gun in Booger Red's hand tilt down and the trigger pulled in that split-second before the gun barrel levelled. Pain like a hot branding iron seared his ribs, twisting him sideways in the saddle.

Booger Red's horrible scream blotted out

the echoes of both guns as the gun dropped from his hand. Both hands clawed at his belly where the .45 slug from Pete's gun had entered. His hat had fallen off as his shaggy head lobbed. Pete watched, the smoking gun tilted in his hand, as the big man doubled over the saddle horn and pitched to the ground. Booger Red Craven was dead before the echoes of his death cry died in the broken badlands.

'What the hell happened to that kid of mine?' Long Tom Savage shouted as he spurred his horse, waving a saddle carbine.

Mitch Moran rode into sight, heading off the lanky ex-convict who had been his cell mate at the Deer Lodge prison. The gun in Mitch's hand spat fire as Long Tom recognized him. Mitch's bullet went into the open mouth and Long Tom Savage went over backwards as his horse whirled.

Mitch Moran sat his horse out in the open. His carbine cracked and one of the renegade cowhands screamed and fell from his horse.

There was a white moon that shed a pale light through the dusk. Mitch's scarred face was revealed in all its horribly maimed hideous detail as he levered smoking shells from his saddle carbine and fresh cartridges into the breech. The stock of the gun never lifted above the line of his cartridge belt as the gun barrel followed a moving target. Whenever his gun spat flame a man was shot from his saddle. Half a dozen guns blazed but Mitch seemed oblivious to the hail of whining bullets around him.

Teal was taking advantage of the situation. He was bent across the saddle horn and along the neck of his running horse as he headed for the broken badlands. The shelter of the high sagebrush and greasewood lay fifty yards ahead when Zee Dunbar, sitting his horse inside the dark shadow of the corral, lined his carbine sights on Teal's back and pulled the trigger. Teal jerked over backwards as the bullet severed his spine. He was dead when his body hit the ground. The horse, empty saddle stirrups popping, reached the brush and was hidden from sight before the first echo of Zee's bushwhacker shot had silenced.

Pete saw the stark murder with a numbed reality. He caught a glimpse of gun flame as Zee Dunbar shot a second time, saw Mitch twist in his saddle as the 30-40 bullet hit him. He was weaving like a drunken man when he spurred his horse back into the high willow thicket.

The gunfire stopped, leaving a tense silence that was charged with danger. Somewhere a man moaned out his final moments on earth.

Pete leaned sideways in his saddle as he

rode back to where Zee Dunbar sat his horse inside the high pole corral. He held his left hand against his ribs, the blood seeping through his fingers. A strange reaction was setting in and he shoved his gun into its holster before it fell from his shaky hand. Cold sweat broke out from every pore as he shivered in the grip of a sudden chill. He felt weak and dizzy and the grey dusk seemed to blacken into night as he rode into the corral.

Zee and his horse were no more than a blurred black shapeless blot. The gun in his hand was concealed behind the fat brown jug.

Pete heard his voice as if it came from a long distance, saying, 'Even a damn lawyer like Steve Costello can outsmart himself. He had it all fixed so Tracy and you would get the Bradded Z when I kicked the bucket. But ol' Zee is a hell of a long ways from bein' dead. But you ain't, Pete. No bald-faced kid can lollywag around with my wife and live to brag about it.'

Zee's words were making sense now as Pete's brain cleared.

'I had it made to kill the pair of you while you were dancin'. Like I got 'er made now.' Zee's eyes were murderous, ugly, insane eyes.

Pete's hand was sweat slimed as he gripped the butt of his holstered gun. He heard the double-click as the whisky-crazed cowman thumbed back the hammer of his six-shooter.

The explosion of a Winchester carbine shattered the night. Zee Dunbar jerked in his saddle and the cocked gun in his hand shattered the fat brown jug that hung from his saddle horn with a muffled sound. The grizzled cowman doubled up like an empty sack and fell slowly from the saddle to lie dead in the puddle of spilled whisky.

Mitch Moran held the smoking saddle gun in his hands as he rode through the gate. The front of his grey flannel shirt was dark with the spreading stain of blood. The pallor of death was on the scarred face, his squinted eyes glazed, as he rode up beside Pete. He let the gun drop to the ground as he held out a blood-smeared hand to touch the law badge pinned to Pete's shirt.

Pete swung to the ground and lifted the dying man from the saddle. The shadows of night erased the bitterness and hate from the scarred face. A twinkle showed through the glaze that filmed the man's eyes as he forced a grin back on his stiffened lips. Mitch Moran died like that in Pete's arms.

Pete pulled the saddles off the two horses and turned them loose. Then he mounted his horse and found the other riderless horses and took off the saddles and bridles, freeing them. He let the dead men lie where they had fallen.

The blood dried and crusted on his bullet-nicked ribs, caking the shirt with a red dust. The pain of the wound was bothersome, a little sickening, and the sight of the sprawled dead around him added to the nausea that came into his throat. No human being afoot or on horseback showed. Peter saw the freshly burned Question Mark road iron on the cattle that was spread out across the river bottom pasture land, hock deep in grass, grazing hungrily.

Somehow, Pete was vaguely aware of the fact that he was now owner of the Bradded Z cow outfit. Zee Dunbar had put his signature to the legal document that Steve Costello had drawn up on the train, leaving everything to young Pete. That was why Zee had tried to kill him.

Ownership of the big cow outfit gave Pete no elation. Pete wanted only this little ranch on the banks of the Misssouri and the Mitch Moran place adjoining it that Zee Dunbar had taken by gun point. Nora would want it that way when they were married. That was all they wanted from the Bradded Z. That much they had both earned.

Steve Costello would attend to everything. Pete would want Old Brocky and Mike, Doctor Cole and Arthur Jackson down for the wedding, with Sheriff Ike Niber and Judge

Dewar. A small quiet wedding with only close friends present.

The stillness of death was in the night's silence as Pete sat alone on the bank of the wide Missouri, waiting for daybreak when Sheriff Ike Niber would show up. Wise in the ways of the cow country and its men, Ike had given those men the chance to settle their own lawless feud that had been of long standing.

Pete had found what he needed in the cabin. Clean bandages and clean clothes. He had stripped to the hide and sat there in the river washing the dried sweat and crusted blood off, toweling dry and wrapping a tight bandage to bind the bullet rips along his ribs. He had made a pot of coffee and carried the blackened coffee-pot and a battered tin cup to the river bank. Dressed in clean dry clothes he sat cross-legged in the shadow of the brush, a carbine across his lap, drinking the strong hot coffee, rolling and smoking cigarettes. The pain in his ribs had slacked off to a dull ache as he sat there with a stoic Indian-like patience of a deer stalker, waiting and listening for the little sounds no man could hear. The voice of the night itself and the whisper of the river as it revealed its secrets to its banks. It was a long time in coming. Man's violence had torn the ageless, peaceful quiet apart with ruthless blasphemy of voice and gun.

The utter exhaustion was slowly claiming the weary muscles and easing the taut nerves when the little sounds crept into the innermost part of the man who was blessed with that rare gift to a chosen few.

A whitetail doe with a spotted fawn came out on the sandbar to drink. A muskrat came from its hole in the clay bank and swam across the moonlit surface of the water, leaving a fan-like ripple behind. Below, an old grey-muzzled beaver came down its slide, the slap of its wide tail sounding that the night was safe from man's danger. The boom of a horned owl passed it along through the cottonwoods. The waters of the old river commenced an endless saga, a low-chanted requiem for those men who had died.

It gave a promise of a boy's dream come true, fulfilled beyond all expectation to the man who sat in a listening understanding. Slowly, gently, the sounds of the night and the river came to heal the hurts.

Nora Moran, who had come with Sheriff Ike Niber, found Pete Walters asleep on the river bank as the dawn of a new day was born. Her lips brushed the smile on the man's lips and Pete awoke to the sunlight that shone bravely through the tears that filmed her eyes.